PUFFIN BOOKS

MR TEAGO AND THE MAGIC SLIPPERS

It was Mr Teago's birthday and Martha did so want to get him a pair of slippers, but she couldn't find any anywhere – at least not for the right sort of money. In the end she had to make do with a box, quite a pretty box, but only a box all the same. Imagine her surprise then when the box turns out to hold a splendid pair of blue and gold slippers with strangely curved toes and an even stranger effect on the wearer.

Entanglements in tea-towels and petticoats, Great Aunts in distress, flying scarecrows, encounters with Chinese sorcery, and possibilities of Immediate Destruction are just some of the problems that Martha has to face as a result of her odd purchase.

Martha and Mr Teago's hilarious adventures and mishaps make a delightful and highly entertaining story that will be especially enjoyed by younger readers.

Imogen Chichester

Mr Teago
and the Magic Slippers

Illustrated by Charlotte Voake

PUFFIN BOOKS

Puffin Books, Penguin Books Ltd, Harmondsworth, Middlesex, England
Penguin Books, 40 West 23rd Street, New York, New York 10010, U.S.A.
Penguin Books Australia Ltd, Ringwood, Victoria, Australia
Penguin Books Canada Ltd, 2801 John Street, Markham, Ontario, Canada L3R 1B4
Penguin Books (N.Z.) Ltd, 182–190 Wairau Road, Auckland 10, New Zealand

First published by Kestrel Books 1983
Published in Puffin Books 1984

Made and printed in Great Britain by
Richard Clay (The Chaucer Press) Ltd, Bungay, Suffolk
Set in Linotype Pilgrim

For Antonia With Love

Contents

chapter 1

The Magic Shop

Martha stood outside the dingy little shop and read for the second time the notice above the door:

> 'Madame Wu' it ran,
> 'Purveyor of Magic
> (Wholesale & Retail)
> Hats
> Rabbits
> Wands, etc.
> always in stock
> Specialist in Oriental Magic
> Early Closing Wednesdays.'

Well, there was no harm in trying! It did at least look rather an interesting sort of shop. She took a deep breath and walked in.

Inside it was very dark, and very small and musty with a peculiar scenty smell that she did not like very much. The walls and ceiling were completely hidden by the myriad things which hung from them: silks and swords and beads and baubles, carved jade and ivory and amber, scrolls and lanthorns and joss-sticks and back-scratchers and little bamboo bird-cages. Martha had never seen such an assortment of wonders.

'Good afternoon,' said a voice behind her, and she turned round to behold a man with a dark-skinned face and a white turban, sitting at a little lacquer table.

'Mr J. Jamboree, at your service,' he said, bowing a
little bow. 'I am Madame Wu's assistant. In what way
can I help you?'

'I want a pair of slippers,' said Martha.

'Ah,' said the man. 'Slippers.'

'Yes,' said Martha. 'Men's slippers, please. Middl-
ing size. And they must be warm and comfortable and
easy to put on, but they mustn't fall off. And they must
be very nice to look at, and they mustn't cost more than
one pound and ninety-seven pence. I didn't quite manage to save two whole pounds.'

'Perhaps you would be better advised to be trying a
shoe shop,' said the man. 'If you were requiring a hat it
would be a simple matter, we are having many many
hats in all sizes, with or without rabbit. Are you quite
sure you are not preferring a hat?'

'I am afraid not,' said Martha. 'I really do want
slippers. And I've tried all the shoe shops, but all the

nice slippers are too expensive and all the cheap ones are too nasty.'

'We are having excellent suits,' said the man, taking a coat-hanger from a hook on the wall and turning it this way and that. 'All sizes too.'

'That's only a coat-hanger,' said Martha.

'Indeed no,' said the man, 'if you will permit me to contradict. It is a suit. The fact that you can only see the coat-hanger merely goes to prove that it is quite invisible to the naked eye, as guaranteed by the maker.' And he pointed to a label tied to the hanger.

'Oh,' said Martha. 'I see. But I really do want a pair of slippers. It's for a present.'

'Wands, now,' said the man. 'We have a very fine selection of wands, though it is really desirable to be a magician to get the best out of a wand. How about silk handkerchiefs?'

'A silk handkerchief certainly would be nice,' said Martha politely, 'only I do really –'

'I am afraid it is not possible to buy one silk handkerchief only, they are sold by the mile, or half-mile, in special cases. All colours.'

'That wouldn't do,' said Martha, beginning to grow a little desperate. 'I do really want slippers. It's for a birthday present, you see, for Mr Teago. He's a friend of mine. And it's his birthday today, so I've absolutely got to find a pair this afternoon. Are you *sure* you haven't got any?'

'Young miss,' said the man apologetically, 'I am truly sorry. In this shop we are having a great assortment of strange and for the most part useless items, and I would with pleasure sell you any which are coming within your small means; indeed, I am most happy to make a reduction in order to be assisting you, for, truth to tell, it is a long time since I am selling anything at all, and Madame Wu is not, alas, the easiest of employers . . . Now, how about a canary? Or an Indian rope? Or a backless, frontless, bottomless box? Collapsible gold-fish bowl? Disappearing turtle-dove? Must it *really* be a pair of slippers?'

'I'm afraid so,' said Martha sadly. She really felt rather sorry for Mr J. Jamboree, he was being so kind and helpful. She began to tell him about Mr Teago, and how he lived at the bottom of the Great Aunts' garden, and how his dear old slippers had grown shabby and how the Great Aunts had thrown them away so that now he had to wear his stiff Sunday boots in the even-ings, which was why it was so important to find him some new ones for his birthday.

'So you see, I've *got* to get him some,' she finished.

'Please be seated,' said Mr Jamboree, who had listened with sympathy. 'I will be having one more look, since you are being so very insistent, though I am of the most positive opinion that there is no such thing in this shop.'

So Martha sat down behind the lacquer table, and while Mr Jamboree was busy pulling down box after box and opening drawer after drawer she entertained him with the history of her life, telling him how she had come to live with Great Aunt May and Great Aunt Beatrice (who were not really her Great Aunts at all, but only her guardians) and of how they had found her in a cardboard box on the doorstep and had thought she was a guinea-pig.

'But when they found I wasn't, they adopted me; but they didn't really like babies very much, so Mrs McConkey looked after me. At first they called me Arthur because I had short hair, so they thought I must be a boy, and then afterwards they had to alter it to Martha. They're very kind, really, only rather strict...'

By this time the tiny shop was filled almost to the ceiling with rabbits and snakes and doves and eggs and cards and coloured handkerchiefs, but alas, no slippers.

'Young miss,' said Mr Jamboree at last, slithering down an Indian rope, 'I am sorry to say that we are having positively no slippers in this shop. But to save myself from any further trouble I have pleasure in offering you any item you are caring to choose, at cost price. Only please be choosing something quickly, for I am having now a great deal of work putting everything back in its proper place before my mistress is waking up. Every day, thanks to a merciful heaven, she is sleeping from two till four, but she is never in a very happy frame of mind when she awakes, though I am not wishing to be disloyal. Choose something quickly, if you please.'

It was very disappointing, but Mr Jamboree had been extremely kind. Martha thanked him for going to such a lot of trouble and looked round hurriedly for anything that might take Mr Teago's fancy.

'What's that?' she asked, pointing to something very high up under the ceiling. 'That red box?'

Mr Jamboree climbed up again and fished the red box off the shelf with the aid of a stick with a boat-hook on the end. 'It is just a box,' he said.

'It's rather pretty,' said Martha, picking it up off the floor and dusting it with her sleeve. It was dark red and had things painted on it all the way round, dragons and flowers. And birds too. Mr Teago was very fond of birds. 'Please may I have it?' she asked.

Mr Jamboree bowed, feeling immensely relieved; and Martha, unzipping her old leather purse, poured

13

the contents into the pink palms of Mr Jamboree's brown hands.

'Young miss,' he said, counting the money, 'you are giving me too much. In my country boxes such as these are given away free to carry home the shopping.' And, keeping one of the silver coins, he gave Martha back the rest. 'In case you are finding what you are looking for elsewhere,' he said.

Then he opened the door for her and she stepped out of the musty little shop into the shining April air, and walked away down the street holding the box very carefully in both hands, but still wishing very much that it had been a pair of slippers.

From the doorway of the shop Mr Jamboree, feeling a little sad, watched her go.

chapter 2

Mr Teago

Martha turned up the alley and let herself in through the garden door in the wall and went down the path to the back door of Number Eleven. In the dark old kitchen, with its homely smell of buns and coffee and paraffin oil, Mrs McConkey dozed peacefully in the basket chair beside the stove, her spectacles on her nose and *Sporting Life* on the floor beside her.

The Great Aunts had evidently not yet returned from their Meeting, for the tea-tray with the silver muffin dish and the fluted cups and saucers stood ready waiting on the table. On the stove the kettle hummed comfortably.

Martha tiptoed through the kitchen and climbed swiftly up the glassy oak stairs that wound their uneven way to her bedroom right at the top. It had been her room ever since she could remember, though Mrs McConkey had told her that when she was a baby she had spent most of her life in the broom-cupboard where the Great Aunts could not hear her. Mrs McConkey said it was a grand wee place right enough, with the shelf at the back that was just handy for a carry-cot and the holes in the door for air, and it saved no end of bother carrying her up and down.

But despite the undoubted charms of the broom-cupboard Martha was glad that she no longer lived there, for she loved her bedroom. It was so high up that from her window she could look over the roofs and see the conker trees in the Cathedral Close, and beyond them the fairy-tale spires and pinnacles of the Cathedral itself, so old and grey and lichen-grown that it seemed as if it had stood there since time began; and indeed, it almost had.

As she looked out of the window now she calculated that Mr Teago would be just pushing his bicycle through the Close; in a minute or two he would come to his favourite seat beneath the chestnut tree and he would stop, propping his bicycle against the trunk; then he would take off his gauntlet gloves and his bee-hat and veil and sit down, fumbling in his pocket for his pipe and his tobacco and his matches...

Mr Teago was really retired; but not wishing to lead an idle life he had applied to the County Council for the post of Honorary Bee-Keeping Adviser, and now spent his days – or at any rate some of his days – in a cosy little office which he shared with the Rodent Officer. There, sitting in front of their good coal fire, drinking numerous cups of dark brown tea provided by the Council, they would talk by the hour about their rats and their bees.

When four o'clock struck they would leave their office and, still talking, walk down miles of green-and-brown corridors till they came to the yard where they kept their bicycles; then they would mount their machines and pedal away, one laden with traps and bait and tins of poison, the other with a hundred bits of beehives. So much equipment did Mr Teago carry that he was obliged to wear quite a lot of it, for want of enough room on the bicycle.

He always looked forward to that moment of the afternoon when he would prop his bicycle against the chestnut tree and sit down on the bench to smoke his pipe, and this afternoon he felt happier than ever. The sun shone, the birds sang and the sweet, strong, earthy smell of spring filled the air. Overhead the chestnut leaves were about to burst out of their sticky brown buds like flights of green parakeets. He puffed contentedly on his pipe, his eyes roaming over his beloved Cathedral.

'Good heavens!' he exclaimed suddenly, taking his pipe out of his mouth, 'I do believe it's my birthday! Good gracious! I believe it is!'

For several minutes he sucked on his pipe and pondered, thinking how odd it was that he didn't feel any older. 'And how old *am* I?' he mused. 'I've quite lost count. Must be – let me see, must be seventy. Good heavens!'

Seventy ... It did sound very old, very old indeed. That meant it must be fifteen years since he first came to live at Number Eleven! Amazing how fast time went as one got older. The years simply whizzed by like telegraph poles seen from a train. *Seventy*!

'Sweet Seventy and never been – well, never been married, at any rate!' He chuckled. He'd come jolly near it, though, from time to time. Nearly been caught by May *and* Beatrice, in fact, and probably would have been if there had only been one of them. Their being twins had saved him: he couldn't have married them both. Not that he had *wanted* to marry either of them but that hadn't put them off in the least; in fact the more reluctant he became the more determined were they. As usual it had been Mrs McConkey who had come to his rescue.

'And wouldn't it be the handiest thing if you was just to share the poor man, and not be tearing him limb from limb between the two of you? And isn't there a grand wee house an' all that'd just be doing him fine, above beyond the rhubarb?'

'Mr Teago could scarcely live in the potting-shed, Mrs McConkey. Be sensible.'

'It's not the potting-shed I'm talking of, sure it's not. Isn't there the beautiful little old railway-carriage that was put there long years ago for a summer-house, and falling to bits for want of use? And wouldn't Mr Teago be just charmed to live there, him being the great gardener that he is?'

And so Mr Teago had moved in, for, being very fond of both rhubarb and railway-carriages, it had suited him perfectly. It was arranged that he should keep the garden tidy and supply the household with fruit, flowers and vegetables. And honey, of course. And in return he was allowed into the house for meals, baths and conversation. It proved an excellent arrangement, satisfactory to all parties.

The greatest and most unexpected joy of his life had turned out to be Martha. Until he met her, Mr Teago had never really known any children, and used to think of them all as noisy, grubby, sticky-fingered little pests. And so it was a great surprise to him to find that he actually looked forward to Martha's visits. He would go to meet her when he heard sounds of her toddling approach, and would entertain her in his carriage, ceremoniously offering her a Parkinson's Humbug from the ancient tin on the luggage-rack.

With these thoughts of Martha, Mr Teago recollected once more that it was his birthday, and he felt all at once absurdly excited. Knocking out his pipe on the edge of the seat he gathered up his belongings, donned his hat and his gauntlet gloves and resumed his journey, pushing the clanking bicycle.

chapter 3

The Birthday Party

'Now!' said Great Aunt Beatrice, creaking to her feet, when at long last supper was over. Birthday or no birthday, Mr Teago had been made to finish all his brussels sprouts, for the Great Aunts had a way of turning any sort of jollification into a lesson in Good Behaviour; even poor Mrs McConkey had been told off for producing a beautiful pink cake and a jelly instead of tapioca and figs.

The cake looked almost too good to eat and, at the same time, too good not to; there were sugar shells and

stars and squiggles all over it, and across the top, in curly sugar writing:

HAPPY BIRTHDAY MR TEAGO
SEVENTY

Martha hoped he would not mind having his age so bluntly proclaimed; a golden blaze of candles, she felt, would have been rather more tactful.

But Mr Teago seemed not to mind at all: indeed he appeared to be highly delighted, and after a while even the Great Aunts had slipped into a good humour.

'Now,' said Great Aunt Beatrice again, when they were all assembled in the sitting-room. 'Presents!'

'Yes, presents!' echoed Great Aunt May, standing beside her sister. Martha, accustomed to seeing them dressed as much like men as was fitting for ladies, thought they looked very odd in the frills and ruffles of their 'concert gowns', worn in honour of the occasion, and could not help staring.

Great Aunt Beatrice held out her present.

'I say!' said Mr Teago, undoing the paper and revealing a brown-and-yellow piece of knitting. 'I say!' He looked a little puzzled.

'And you're to wear it, mind!' said Great Aunt Beatrice waggling her finger at him. 'We don't want any more of those nasty head-colds, do we?'

'Ah!' said Mr Teago, enlightened. 'A balaclava helmet! Just what I wanted. And –' undoing the second present, '– a muffler! By Jove! Awfully good of you, May...'

'Aren't you going to try them on?'

Obediently Mr Teago pulled the balaclava over his head. Muffled sounds came through the wool.

'You have it back to front, dear,' said Great Aunt Beatrice, yanking it round.

Miss May wound the muffler round his neck several times, and Mr Teago began to look very hot. At last, however, he was allowed to take them off, and it was Martha's turn.

Now that the moment she had been waiting for all the evening had arrived, Martha began to wish that it hadn't. If only – if only she had been able to get a pair of slippers, how different she would have felt! But as it was, all she had was a rotten old box, which in some countries would have been given away for nothing . . .

'Manyhappyreturnsoftheday!' she said, in a great rush, holding out the parcel and going very pink in the face. She wished the Great Aunts had not been there.

Mr Teago took it and, sitting down rather heavily on one of the chairs he was not supposed to sit on, opened the card.

'To Mr Teago,' he read, 'With love from Martha.'

> 'I hope your Birthday Presents
> Will be just what you please,
> And I hope your Birthday Supper
> Won't be macaroni cheese.
> I hope you like your Birthday Cake,
> (Mrs McConkey did it bake)
> And I hope you'll like this Indian Box,
> You can use it for your socks.
> I really meant to buy you slippers
> Nothing rhymes with that but kippers!'

'Pooh!' exclaimed the Great Aunts together. 'I don't think much of *that*!'

Mr Teago gave a little wink and started to undo the parcel. Martha hugged herself excitedly, while the

Great Aunts moved closer, disapproving yet inquisitive.

'Gold string!' said one.

'And red paper!' sniffed the other; Martha wished more than ever that they had not been there. Suddenly Mr Teago dropped the whole thing on the floor.

'Oh, my goodness me, how stupid I am!' and he bent down to pick everything up. But the Great Aunts were quicker: like vultures they swooped, each grabbing something that to Martha's amazement had fallen out of the box.

'Slippers!' cried Great Aunt Beatrice.

'Slippers!' cried Great Aunt May.

Martha was speechless with astonishment. Slippers they most certainly were, though where they had come from and how they had got there, she could not possibly imagine. The Great Aunts were holding them up to the electric light, the better to examine them, and Martha could see by the strangely curved toes and the glowing colours that they were no ordinary slippers.

'Where on earth,' said Great Aunt May, 'did she get such things?'

'They're not even worth two curtain-rings!'

'They must have come from the market-place.'

'What an awful thought!'

'It's a real disgrace!'

'One can see they're old.'

'And so shabby, too.'

'And that vulgar gold!'

'And that faded blue!'

'And the size is wrong.'

'And the width's not right.'

'They are far too long.'

'And they're much too tight!'

'They're so out-of-date.'

'And they look so cheap.'

'*I'd* throw them straight on the garbage-heap!'

Martha felt herself going redder and redder in the face till she felt she might be going to burst. Suddenly she could bear it no longer.

'They're not yours!' she cried, flinging herself at the Great Aunts. 'They're Mr Teago's and they're for his birthday and I got them specially for him and they're *his*!' And she snatched the slippers away and thrust them into Mr Teago's hands. Furiously she glared from Great Aunt to Great Aunt, then, bursting into a flood of tears, she rushed out of the room.

chapter 4

How Mr Teago Tried on the Slippers

All next day Martha was punished.

First she had to write out fifty times in her best writing: 'I must show Respect to My Elders and Betters.' Then, 'I must not buy Second-Hand Goods'; and after that she had to let down her last summer's school uniform. When that was done, she was made to learn by heart a long and dreadful poem entitled 'The Wilful Orphan' that Great Aunt Beatrice had written herself:

> O, witness the Ingratitude,
> The Hair Unkempt, the Manners Rude,
> The Face Unwashed, th'Untidy Room,
> The Undarned Socks, the Unused Broom;
>
> The Gross Unpunctuality,
> The Unrefined Hilarity,
> The Wicked, Wanton Wastefulness
> And Lack of Genteel Tastefulness;
>
> The Total Lack of Interest
> In Everything considered Best
> For Cultivation of the Mind;
> The Place in Class: far, far behind.

There were seven more verses all in the same vein, ending with the lines:

Poor Foster-Parents, Gen'rous, Mild,
Who sheltered this Ungrateful Child,
Rewarded at the Last shall be
For Patience, Love and Charity.

Not until tea-time did Martha finish all the tasks the Great Aunts could think up. Wearily she opened the scullery door and walked up the gravel path to Mr Teago's railway-carriage. She sat down upon the green wooden seat labelled Diddlecombe Junction and waited for him to return from work.

Martha often wished that she could have lived with Mr Teago instead of in the proper house, but there was not really room for more than one person, even though the wall had been knocked down between two compartments to make a bigger sitting-room. The Non-Smoker was the bedroom.

As she waited her eyes wandered about the little lawn; Mr Teago always cut it with shears for fear of upsetting the bees with the noise of the mower. Each beehive was painted a different colour, and its name was neatly printed in pokerwork on a little sign nailed to the roof: Jasmine, Forgetmenot, Lavender, Rose and Primrose. Jasmine was white. In every corner of the garden grew the plants that the bees liked best, for Mr Teago always said that they worked better for you if you worked for them. He spent a lot of time talking to them, and always informed them of everything of importance.

And then there were the birds, for Mr Teago loved them almost as much as he loved his bees, and he filled the garden with little luxuries for them, so that wherever you looked there were bird-baths or bird-tables or nesting-boxes or dangling coconut shells; indeed, Martha believed that if Mr Teago could have made nests for them too he would have done so: as it was he was forever collecting useful-looking pieces of horse-hair and moss. Even the scarecrow standing among the young peas seemed to hold out his stick arms specially for the birds to perch on.

But even with all these things to look at Martha found after a while that she could not sit still any longer, for time goes so dreadfully slowly when you are waiting that it often seems to have stopped altogether. She decided to go and look for Mr Teago.

She saw him from quite a long way off, sitting on the bench in the Close, smoking his pipe and gazing vacantly at the Cathedral. He turned and waved when she called his name.

'I've escaped,' she said sitting on the seat beside him.

'By Jove,' said Mr Teago, taking his pipe out of his mouth. 'Won't they be cross?'

Martha thought they probably would be; but since they'd been cross all day it really wouldn't make much difference.

'That's too bad,' said Mr Teago, '*Too* bad! And all because of me. Poor Martha. And I never had a chance to thank you for my present, or for the splendid card. I like the poem very much.' He stood up and patted his pockets and felt inside his coat, but after a while he sat down again.

'Stupid of me,' he muttered. 'Must have left it in the office. I wrote one for you, too, to thank you.'

'Couldn't you just recite it?' asked Martha.

Mr Teago was doubtful if he could remember it all, but nevertheless he stood up and cleared his throat.

'My dear little Martha
You know I'd much rather
Have thanked you at once for my beautiful shoes;
But your excellent Aunts
With their Cans and their Can'ts
Made me wisely remember my Ps and my Qs!

To have thanked you in person
Had made matters worse'n
They already are for both you and for me;
So I'm writing this rhyme,
For I've plenty of time,
Though of talent, alas, I have none, as you see.

Such splendiferous shoes
Of such glorious hues
I never before in my life have possessed!
So I'll not care a fig –
For Aunt Thingamejig –

Oh dear, I'm afraid I've forgotten the rest!'

'Oh, that's *awfully* good!' cried Martha, highly delighted. 'You're an absolute *poet*!'

'No, no, no, not at all,' said Mr Teago, modestly. 'But they really are the most capital slippers. I don't think I ever saw a pair like them. Ernest was very envious!' (Ernest was the Rodent Officer.)

'Did you take them to the office, then?'

'Of course; Miss Twisset admired them too. The tea-lady, you know.'

'Do they fit all right?' asked Martha.

'Perfectly,' said Mr Teago. 'Might have been made for me. Would you like to see? There's no one looking.'

He bent down and untied his boot-laces while Martha fished the slippers out of the old canvas haversack he called his Bee-bag.

'The funny thing,' said Martha, 'is that I couldn't get any slippers. You see, I really only bought the box. I didn't know there was anything inside it. You don't think I ought to return the slippers, do you?'

'Well,' said Mr Teago, considering, 'if they didn't know there was anything inside the box, they're not going to miss them, are they? I think it's all right. I hope so, anyway!'

He wriggled his long feet in the thin silk socks and stuck them into the slippers, using his finger as a shoe-horn. 'They're a little bit tight to get *on*,' he said, 'but once you're in they're a capital fit. There!' He lifted his right foot off the ground, the better to admire it. Up and up he lifted it, turning it from side to side. It certainly was very handsome, and an excellent fit. For some minutes they both gazed at it admiringly.

'Someone's coming,' said Martha. 'You'd better put it down.'

But he seemed not to hear, and the lady and

gentleman strolling by looked rather strangely at the respectable figure of Mr Teago reclining on a Cathedral bench with one leg in the air.

'Really!' said the lady, looking back indignantly. 'He very nearly kicked my hat off! Wasn't it that funny little Bee-man?'

'Can't say I noticed his face,' said the gentleman. 'Got a good look at his feet, though. Dash me if the fellow wasn't wearing his bedroom slippers!'

'How very peculiar!' said the lady. 'Perhaps he is a little *odd*, don't you know.'

Martha, hearing this conversation, went very red in the face; she didn't like Mr Teago being called a 'funny little Bee-man'. She hoped no more people would come along.

'Mr Teago! You must sit up! And put your foot on the ground! Did you *hear* those people?'

But instead of doing as she said Mr Teago began to lift his other foot up as well, up and up until they were both floating in the air at eye-level, and Mr Teago – well, Mr Teago was almost horizontal.

'You must be *tremendously* strong,' said Martha, astonished. 'However do you do it?' And sitting down on the bench beside him she tried to do it too, but even when she pushed against the seat with her hands she could not raise her feet more than about eighteen inches.

'I think I'd better be going back,' she said, letting her feet fall to the ground. 'Otherwise I'll probably be punished all tomorrow as well. Why don't you put your feet down?'

'That,' said Mr Teago, in a very upside-down sort of voice, 'is what I simply can't make out: they don't seem to want to come! Perhaps if you were to catch them, my dear, we might be able to bring them down together, er, as it were.'

So Martha caught hold of Mr Teago's right ankle and pulled it earthwards, and, bending his knee, set his foot properly on the gravel path.

'There!' she said, and reached for the other one. But alas! No sooner had she got the left one down than the right one was up again, and as soon as she let go of the left one it sailed away to join its fellow.

'Oh goodness! What *are* we going to do?'

'Perhaps if you could catch them both at the same time my dear ...' said Mr Teago apologetically. 'I am sorry to put you to so much bother. It's really very foolish of me – I don't know what's the matter with me at all.'

'Oh, dear!' cried Martha, more upset than ever. 'It's not *you* that's the matter. It's the *slippers*! I should have known there was something odd about them the way they just appeared like that! Oh, poor Mr Teago! I'm terribly sorry. We'd better take them off at once.'

But this proved to be easier said than done, for even after Martha had captured both Mr Teago's feet she could not pull the slippers off: in some extraordinary way they seemed to have grown smaller, or else Mr Teago's feet had grown larger, it was hard to say which. Mr Teago held on to the bench with both hands and Martha held on to his left foot, and they tugged and tugged until, at last, off came the slipper.

'Whew! That's one,' said Martha, picking herself up off the gravel. 'They must be *dreadfully* uncomfortable!'

'No,' said Mr Teago, 'not in the least. That's another very odd thing ... They are truly the most remarkable slippers! Most remarkable! I wonder what would have happened if I had been standing up?'

chapter 5

How Martha Met the Chinawoman

That night Martha lay awake for a long time thinking of the slippers and of all the queer things about them: of how they made Mr Teago's feet go sailing into the air, and of how difficult they had been to get off, and of how they had appeared so mysteriously out of what had certainly been an empty box.

This last factor worried her considerably; for she felt that she had not really paid for the slippers, Mr Jamboree having given back nearly all her money. She decided to return to the Magic Shop and pay for them as soon as possible. Perhaps she might be able to find out some more about them at the same time. What, for instance, did that foreign-looking writing mean, woven into the sole? Did it just say Size Nine? or could it possibly be Directions for Use?

Because there certainly ought to be some Directions. It was all very nice and exciting and all that, having a pair of slippers that turned you upside-down, but how about when you wanted to be the right way up? How did you turn the magic off? All she had been looking for, after all, was a comfortable pair of slippers for Mr Teago to wear in the evenings, but he was not going to be very comfortable standing on his head; and besides, what would the Great Aunts say?

So, the next afternoon, when the Great Aunts were rehearsing for the Pageant, one being Boadicea and the other Britannia, and when Mrs McConkey was having forty winks, Martha set out for the Magic Shop, carrying Mr Teago's slippers in their red-painted box.

She had some trouble finding the shop, and it was quite late when, at last, she saw the sign. She opened the door and stepped inside.

The shop seemed darker and mustier than ever and it took some time for her eyes to become accustomed to the gloom, so that at first she thought it was empty. She could see no sign of Mr Jamboree.

Then with a start she became aware of a pair of eyes watching her from the darkest corner of the shop – two bright black eyes set in a face as smooth and yellow as ivory . . .

'Oh!' said Martha, with a jump. 'Good afternoon! I – I didn't see you.'

The person in the corner said nothing, nor did she move, which made Martha wonder if she had made a mistake. Perhaps it was not Madame Wu, after all, but a waxwork figure? She did not know quite how to proceed.

'I – I just came back,' she said at last, addressing the waxwork as there was no one else to talk to, 'I just came back to pay the rest of the money, because you see I only paid for the box because I didn't know they were inside it, but I *would* have if I had known, but anyway I've come back to pay for them now. The slippers, I mean.' She unzipped her purse and an avalanche of coins poured on to the table, rolling in all directions. 'And please,' she went on, kneeling down and retrieving several pennies that had rolled on to the floor, 'will you tell me what the writing says, on the bottom?'

She put the coins back in the heap on the table and opened the red box and took out a piece of tissue-paper,

33

and then another and then another . . . and then a green piece and then a pink piece, then an orange piece and then a red one and then purple and then blue and then another white piece and – 'Oh goodness!' cried Martha, 'I'm sure there wasn't all this paper when I wrapped them up!' And still more and more paper kept coming out of the box, and then wood shavings! Myriads and myriads of little wooden ringlets, more and more and more, until the shop was half filled with them.

'I'm terribly sorry!' cried Martha, overcome with embarrassment. 'I never put them in, really I didn't.'

And then suddenly they stopped, and there were the slippers just as she had packed them, heel-to-toe in the bottom of the box.

There was a sudden rustling of silk and out of the

wide sleeve of her robe shot the Chinawoman's hand, dry and papery as a chrysalis.

'Where—*where* you get these?' she demanded, snatching up the slippers and examining them closely under the little green-shaded lamp. 'How you find them? Tell me!'

'Why, I got them here,' said Martha, surprised, and also somewhat alarmed. 'Mr Jamboree sold them to me the other day. Mr J. Jamboree. At least, he sold me the box. He didn't really sell me the slippers because he didn't know they were there, that's why I came back. To pay for them. I told you. And please can you tell me what the writing says on the bottom?'

But Madame Wu did not answer. In fact she did not even seem to have heard, and Martha thought she was behaving in a very strange manner altogether. She was leaning back in her chair, rocking backwards and forwards with the slippers clasped in her arms, crooning to herself in a funny high-pitched voice that seemed to come out of her nose and made all her Rs sound like Ls. Martha caught a stray word here and there but could not really understand what the Chinawoman was saying – there seemed to be quite a lot about marvels and miracles and that sort of thing.

'Oh, wonder of wonders! Marvel of ancient sorcelors! Pliceless Tleasure of Chinese Empelors—'

'But *please*, what does it *say*?' she interrupted. It seemed likely that Madame Wu might go on like this for quite a long time and it was growing late. 'Please,' she repeated. 'After all, I have paid for them.'

The Chinawoman stopped rocking and sat absolutely still and her little black eyes narrowed to the merest slits in her ivory face. Suddenly she swept Martha's entire fortune off the table with her sleeve.

'Ha!' she said, as the coins flew away into the farthest corners and were lost among the wood shavings. 'Ignorant brat!' (It sounded like Ignolant Blat.) 'You think chickenfeed pay for slippers of my ancestors? Slippers brought by merchants on ancient Silk-Route, all across Roof of World to Court of Emperor and given to noble ancestor for saving life of favourite concubine? Slippers in Wu family since Tang Dynasty until coming of idiot Jamboree . . . Pick up miserable pocket-money and go! GO!'

'NO!' said Martha. 'I won't! Not without the slippers. And I *did* buy them. If you didn't want to sell them they shouldn't have been in the shop. And anyway I don't believe they're very valuable – my Great Aunts didn't think they were very valuable at all. And you still haven't told me what's written on the bottom.'

'What's litten on bottom,' mocked the Chinawoman, in what sounded to Martha rather a nasty voice: she began to feel a bit frightened. But Madame Wu only turned and held the slipper with the writing close to the light, and read:

'Abdullah & Wives
Street of the Carpet-Weavers
Baghdad
By appointment to
His Supreme Magnificence
The Caliph.'

'Street of the *Carpet-Weavers*!' repeated Martha. 'How funny. Why not Shoe-makers?'

But Madame Wu did not answer. She was leaning back as before, her eyes closed, the slippers clasped to her bony Chinese chest. She began the rocking business again.

Martha saw her opportunity, and with a sudden lunge she grabbed the slippers and made for the door, and ran out into the fresh air and away down the little cobbled streets, to left and to right, running faster than she had ever run in her life; nor did she stop until she was once more safe and sound in Mrs McConkey's kitchen.

chapter 6

How Mr Teago Spent an Exciting Evening

That evening happened to be the Annual Dinner of the Cathedral Ladies Bowls Club, and at seven o'clock sharp the Great Aunts left the house, looking very smart and awe-inspiring in their white blazers and hats. Mrs McConkey opened the front door for them and they marched briskly away down the street, in time but out of step. From her bedroom window Martha watched them until they were out of sight, then she ran downstairs to the kitchen.

'Whose turn is it?' she asked.

'Sure and isn't it yours?' said Mrs McConkey. 'Wasn't it the spaghetti we had the last time?'

When the Great Aunts were out Martha and Mr Teago and Mrs McConkey always had supper together in the kitchen, which was much cosier than the dining-room. Martha and Mr Teago took it in turns to do the cooking so that Mrs McConkey should have a rest; when Mr Teago cooked, they had spaghetti, which was his favourite dish, and when Martha cooked they had baked beans. And afterwards Mrs McConkey would make a Nice Pot of Tea and tell their fortunes.

Martha loved these evenings, and indeed so did Mr Teago and Mrs McConkey, all the more, perhaps, because of the feeling that they were doing something slightly wicked. They had to remember not to laugh too loudly in case they should not hear the key turning in the lock when the Great Aunts returned, but this evening they knew they would be undisturbed for a long time: the Cathedral Ladies had healthy appetites.

'Is it looking for your fine new slippers you are?' asked Mrs McConkey, as Mr Teago came into the kitchen in his gardening boots. 'They're here in front of the fire, where Martha's just after leaving them for you. It'll be a treat to see you with something decent on your feet. Come in, now, and sit down, and let's have a look at you!'

Mr Teago looked at Martha. 'Will it be all right, do you think?' he asked uncertainly.

'Sure and why wouldn't it?' said Mrs McConkey. 'It'd be better than them old boots of yours, that should have been given to charity a twelve-month ago, and that's for certain! And don't you go talking to Martha or it's burning the toast again she'll be, or me name's not Maggie McConkey. Come on, now!'

So Mr Teago sat down and took off his boots and rather apprehensively put on the slippers. Mrs McConkey was in raptures.

'Oh, the softness of them! And the fit! And the fine beautiful colours of them and the gold! Why, Martha, 'tis fit for an Earl they are! And when you've done burning every bit of bread in the house will you come and take a look at the fine feet of him!'

At last Martha succeeded in making three pieces of toast, but by this time Mr Teago's feet had unfortunately taken off again and were hovering about six inches above the hearth-rug. Mr Teago was looking worried. Martha took in the situation at a glance.

'Let's move the table over to the fire!' she said,

seizing it and dragging it right up to Mr Teago. A second later there came a fearful crash as his feet swung upwards.

'Mercy on us!' cried Mrs McConkey, picking up the tomato sauce. (When the Great Aunts were out Martha had tomato sauce on everything she possibly could.) 'Is it all the delft in the place you're trying to smash?'

Mr Teago felt very embarrassed, and Martha, very nervous, but as Mr Teago's feet were now nicely jammed beneath the table the rest of the meal passed without further mishap.

'I'll clear the table,' said Martha, 'and then will you tell fortunes? *Please*, Mrs McConkey!'

'Wheedling wee divil, you,' said Mrs McConkey. 'Well, I might. I'm not in the mood for the cards, but I'll tell the tea-leaves, only first we'll be moving the table back to where it belongs, for it's roasted I am like a leg o' mutton, sitting here on top of the stove . . .' and so saying she grasped the table and dragged it back to the middle of the room, leaving Mr Teago stranded upon the basket chair with his legs stuck stiffly out before him. With the weight of the table no longer on top of them they immediately began to rise into the air, and in less than half a minute he was nearly upside down.

'Saints and Martyrs!' shrieked Mrs McConkey from the other side of the table. 'Will you take a look at the man, standing on his head in my kitchen like one o' them Yogi fellows!'

Martha rushed in from the scullery.

'I'm so sorry,' said Mr Teago in a strangled sort of voice. 'I really do apologize! Oh dear, oh dear ...' Unable to hold on to the chair any longer he let go and floated away towards the ceiling.

'Mr Teago!' said Mrs McConkey firmly, 'Will you be after coming down this very minute! I'll not be having any o' them heathenish acrobatics in my kitchen, I'm telling you. It's coming down you are this instant!'

But at that very moment Mr Teago collided with the electric light, and with a flash and a crash and a tinkle of broken glass the kitchen was plunged into darkness.

'Quick!' cried Martha. 'Light a candle, Mrs McConkey! We mustn't lose him, whatever we do! Are you all right, Mr Teago?'

'I think so,' came Mr Teago's voice from somewhere over their heads. 'I think so; only I'm not quite sure of my whereabouts.'

Mrs McConkey struck a match and found the stump of an old candle in the jam-cupboard; by its light they could discern Mr Teago hovering just beneath the ceiling.

'We must get him down,' said Martha, very seriously. 'We'll have to catch his feet or something.'

'It's really rather pleasant when you get used to it,' said Mr Teago, drifting round the kitchen. 'I think I'm getting better at it: look! I can almost steer!' and with gathering speed he zoomed across the room, banked steeply to avoid the fly-paper and slowed down over the sink where he hovered for a little while, rising and falling gently. 'You get a very good lift over the stove,' he said, gliding away in that direction. 'It's the hot air, of course. Rises. Ouch!' He rubbed his head and altered course for the scullery.

'Shut the door!' shouted Martha. 'If he gets out of the kitchen we might never see him again. We've *got* to catch him!'

She scrambled on to the table while Mrs McConkey climbed up on the kitchen stool, but by this time Mr Teago had got up quite a turn of speed and was whizzing round and round the kitchen with outstretched arms, making loud buzzing noises as he went. Strings of onions, bunches of thyme, of sage and dill and rosemary, all went flying.

'Brrrrrrr!' he cried, by now completely out of control and enjoying himself hugely; 'Wheeeeeeee! Yeee-eeeoooooooowww!'

In the midst of all this hullabaloo the kitchen door suddenly flew open, and there – there stood the Great Aunts, looking fiercer than ever in their brass-buttoned uniforms. Martha gaped at them, appalled.

'Oh, Saints in Heaven!' cried Mrs McConkey as she caught sight of them. '*Mr Teago*, will you come down this minute!'

'*What* is the meaning of this?' boomed Great Aunt Beatrice in an awful tone. At the sound of her voice Mr Teago glanced backwards over his shoulder and, going off course, side-slipped across the kitchen straight into the clothes-airer, and there he stuck, in a hopeless entanglement of tea-towels and petticoats.

'Grab him by the feet!' hissed Martha to Mrs McConkey. 'We've got to get the slippers off.'

'*Timothy*!' cried the Great Aunts both together. 'What in the world do you think you're doing. And what has happened to the electricity?'

'It isn't his fault, honestly it isn't,' said Martha, struggling with one slipper while Mrs McConkey worked away at the other; in some extraordinary way they seemed tighter than ever. 'I'm afraid it's – it's *these* . . .' And off they came.

'Those slippers!' said Great Aunt Beatrice. 'I might have known it. I knew we should never have allowed them in the house. I said so at the time and I say it again. Come, May!' And picking the slippers off the kitchen table they marched away with them, holding them carefully at arm's length as if expecting them to go off like fireworks.

chapter 7

Mr Jamboree Has an Inspiration...

The following afternoon, as soon as Madame Wu had retired for her siesta, Mr Jamboree collapsed on to the chair behind the lacquer table and leaned his head on his arm. Never, since he first came to work for the

Chinawoman, could he remember a more frightening morning than the one he had just spent, for Madame Wu's fury was like the fury of a python, cold and deadly. Just to think of it made his knees knock together under the table.

Of course, he had expected it: from the moment that that child had come into the shop asking for a pair of slippers he had had a feeling of impending calamity, though why, exactly, he could not say. There had been nothing very special about that old box, as far as he could remember, in fact it had seemed a perfectly ordinary old box; and it had certainly been empty. Of that he was positive.

But now it seemed that he had committed the most terrible crime: had wilfully sold for a pittance Madame Wu's great-great-grandfather's priceless Persian slippers, made hundreds of years ago from a piece of some fabulous carpet that was said to have magical properties. Magical properties indeed! Didn't everything in this shop have Magical Properties? What about the fifteen dustbin bags of wood shavings that he had spent the morning sweeping up? What were they if not magical? Where had they come from, he would like to know. And the bother he had every day with all the animals and birds appearing and disappearing ... Oh, what with one thing and another Mr Jamboree was heartily sick of magic. It was the cause of all the trouble.

And now he was faced with the impossible task of retrieving the wretched slippers, and how he was to do that he could not begin to think. In fact there was only one clear thought in Mr Jamboree's head as he sat in the stuffy little shop and that was that he would suffer the most fearful punishments if the slippers were not in Madame Wu's hands by sunset on the morrow. He saw himself in a rat-filled cellar, water dripping on his head and sharpened match-sticks being forced under his finger-nails, while a great cauldron of boiling oil hissed and bubbled like a giant chip-pan ... Oh, horrors! What was he to do?

If he had only known the surname of the child, or where she lived, but he had never thought of asking. He knew she was called Martha, and that she had a friend with a name like Sago or Teapot or something, who liked birds and who had had a birthday the day before yesterday; and he knew that she had two great aunts and a person called Mrs MacSomebody. That was all. How, *how* was he going to find a pair of slippers he had never seen and which he did not believe even existed, which belonged – if they *did* exist – to a man whose name he could not remember, who lived at an address he did not know? Surely nobody, since the time of the Arabian Nights, had ever had such an impossible task.

Suddenly he sat up and clutched his turban with both hands.

'That's it!' he cried aloud. 'That is truly, absolutely it! The Arabian Nights! Oh, goodness gracious, why am I not thinking of it before? It is perfectly obvious. I will merely go from house to house as did the wicked uncle in the tale of Aladdin, crying "New Lamps for Old! New Lamps for Old!" Only shoes, of course, not lamps. It may possibly work. At any rate, it is worth trying, and it is anyway the only plan I am likely to be able to think of, though to be truthful,' he added sadly, 'I am not holding out very much hope of succeeding.'

chapter 8

. . . and Makes a Discovery

And so it came about that the next afternoon a very weary Mr Jamboree stood outside the back door of Number Eleven, carrying a bulging, battered suitcase borrowed from a friend in the market. Slung about him were several objects too large to fit into the case, including several polo-sticks and a hatstand. They were rather cumbersome to carry around, but Mr Jamboree hoped they would prove an attraction.

'Good-day, madam,' he said, as Mrs McConkey opened the door. Smiling disarmingly, he stepped quickly into the scullery before she could stop him. 'Good-day,' he said again, flinging open the suitcase. 'May I possibly be interesting you in my most excellent very wide range of indispensable household articles? Yes, please?' He spoke in a very quick clipped fashion, pronouncing it 'Yezz blizz.'

Mrs McConkey frowned. She disapproved of what she called 'them encyclopedia fellows' who came to the door trying to make you buy dozens of enormous books about everything under the sun from aspidistras to zeppelins. As if there wasn't enough to read in the paper! Mrs McConkey didn't hold with such people.

'And what would I be wanting with them old frippery things?' she demanded. 'Will you take them out of me scullery this minute?' And she advanced towards him with a broom.

Mr Jamboree, however, stood his ground and, taking no notice of Mrs McConkey or the broom, began a stream of patter, pulling article upon article out of his seemingly bottomless case:

'... brand-new reversible left-handed peeler? Rotary opener? Foam-rubber kneeler? Boot-brushes, tooth-brushes, hairbrushes, soap? Hearthrug or coal-scuttle? Clothes-line or rope? All-purpose, oven-proof, earth-enware dish, equally useful for meat or for fish? Sponge-rack or plate-rack or toast-rack or tongs? Coat-hangers, crook-whangers, bangers for gongs? Egg-timer? Pump-primer? Two dozen pegs? Foldable airer with optional legs? Pan-scrapers, soap-savers, any-size plugs? Spare lids for saucepans or handles for jugs? Pointer for milk-bottles –'

'NO THANK YOU!' shouted Mrs McConkey, finally managing to get a word in as he paused for breath. 'Not today.' But before she could say another word he was off again, as fast as before:

'But if you're wishing not to buy I'm offering with pleasure the highest market price for goods that you no longer treasure, highest prices paid for goods of china, glass or plastic! Curtains, carpets, underwear – with or without elastic; clothing, footwear: boots and shoes, felt or carpet slippers; sandals, plimsolls, dancing-pumps, even rubber flippers! For carpet slippers specially our price is hard to beat: I beg you, madam, earnestly to cash in on your feet!' He paused for breath again, and sighed. 'I am clearly seeing, madam,' he went on after a minute, 'that you are not having anything worth selling, not even any gentlemen's slippers as I am mentioning before, or you would at once be snapping up my most generous Once-in-a-Lifetime, Never-to-be-Repeated Offer ...' And he shook his head sadly and began to shovel everything back into the suitcase again.

'We've a pair of gentlemen's slippers right enough,' said Mrs McConkey, slightly nettled by the encyclopedia fellow's tone, 'and a fine pair they are an' all, but it's not mine they are to be buying and selling, and indeed, haven't the mistresses them locked away since yesterday evening. But it's all for the best if you ask me, for there's no telling what may happen next with them things, stringing poor Mr Teago up by the heels and smashing the electrics! Ah, but that's the way of the world!'

From this rigmarole Mr Jamboree fastened on one small word that told him his search was over. ' "*Teago*" are you saying? *Mr Teago*? Is he living here in this house?'

chapter 9

How Great Aunt May Gave Way to Curiosity

While Mr Jamboree was haranguing Mrs McConkey in the scullery the Great Aunts were sitting pleasantly on either side of the fireplace in the drawing-room, enjoying the afternoon sunshine and busying themselves with their work, Great Aunt May with her gros-point and Great Aunt Beatrice with her crewel.

The sun and the fire being both rather warm, from time to time they would doze off, their hands dropping into their laps and wools, needles, thimbles slithering soundlessly on to the carpet. For a few moments there would be a gentle snoring and then with a little jolt they would awake, retrieve their bits and pieces and resume their labours. Neither of them would ever admit to having been asleep.

This afternoon, Miss May, recovering from one of these little lapses and her sister being still – well, not exactly awake, found her thoughts turning to the extraordinary goings-on in the kitchen the night before. Of course, it had been quite dark and impossible to see exactly what was happening, but it did *seem* as if Timothy were actually flying round the kitchen! Oh, it must have been just one of his pranks, but all the same Mrs McConkey should really never have allowed it. Beatrice had been quite angry! And Martha had been dreadfully over-excited: she kept saying that it was something to do with the slippers! How perfectly ridiculous! How could it possibly have been?

Great Aunt May stitched away industriously for a few minutes until she had completed the pink bit she was doing; then, Beatrice being still asleep, she thought she might just take a little look at the slippers. She got out of her armchair and stole quietly across the room, opened the top drawer of the bureau and, taking them out, tiptoed back again. Comfortably settled in her chair once more she turned the slippers over in her hands.

When you looked at them closely they were really rather fine, although of course somewhat worn with age. But they seemed much handsomer than she had thought the first time she saw them, the night of Timothy's birthday. and the insides were of scarlet silk, *real* silk, such as one seldom saw nowadays, and the colours, though faded, were still clear ... Almost without realizing what she was doing Great Aunt May removed her right shoe with the toe of her left one and slipped her stockinged foot into Mr Teago's slipper.

Awaking with a start, Great Aunt Beatrice was surprised to behold her sister lying almost prone in her armchair on the other side of the fireplace, with one leg stuck stiffly up in the air and a rather large expanse of pink bloomer exposed to view.

'May! For goodness sake! Whatever can you be thinking of? Sit up, dear, and pull down your skirt. Why, I can see – I can see, well ... *Do* sit up, dear.'

'Oh dear, oh dear,' said Miss May, from the depths of the armchair, 'I would if I could. You'll have to help me. Catch hold of my foot, please, Beatrice.'

'Your *foot*! Whatever use would that be?'

'Please, Beatrice, do catch hold of it. It's the – it's the slipper!'

'So that's it, is it,' said Great Aunt Beatrice, with awful disapproval. 'I might have guessed! Why could you not leave them alone, May, instead of waiting until I was – er, busy with my embroidery? Do try and put your foot down, dear, for Heaven's sake. Someone might *see*.'

'But Beatrice, I *can't*,' said poor Miss May, 'until you get hold of the slipper. It seems to float about all by itself. It is a most peculiar sensation.'

'Now, May,' said Miss Beatrice, 'you're being perfectly ridiculous. How could it possibly be the slipper? Look, I'll put the other one on myself to show you.' And so saying, she bent down and picked the other slipper up off the floor ...

chapter 10

Mr Jamboree Comes to the Rescue

Mr Jamboree, having been ejected from the house by Mrs McConkey, paused for a moment to consider his next move. He was quite sure, now, that he had found the right house, but he still did not know how he was to lay his hands on the slippers. It was clearly no good trying the old housekeeper again, but perhaps he might have more luck with the Mistresses she had spoken of. After all, if they did not want the slippers lying about in the house perhaps they might be willing to sell them. Picking up the suitcase, prawning-net, polo sticks and hatstand, he let himself out of the garden door and walked down the alley towards the street.

Outside the front door he set everything down, straightened his turban, did one or two practice smiles and knocked briskly. After a few minutes, nobody having come to the door, he knocked again. Still no one came. He began to think that the house must be empty: perhaps Mrs McConkey had gone out into the garden. Bending down, he put his ear to the letter-box. There was certainly more than one person in the house: quite loud sounds of habitation issued from within. He listened harder.

'What did I tell you, Beatrice?' came a voice. 'And you wouldn't believe me.'

'Well, you had no right to get them out in the first place, May. They were put there for a purpose.'

'I've said I'm sorry. Oh, dear, I do wish Mrs McConkey would come. You call her, Beatrice.'

'It's no good, she never hears. You'll have to ring the bell. You're nearest.'

'You know I can't, dear. I can't sit up.'

'You can do it with your toe, can't you?'

Mr Jamboree was by this time very curious to know what was going on in the room from which this strange conversation seemed to be coming. He moved over to the window and peered through the glass, shutting out the reflected light with his hand. Inside he could vaguely make out two stout elderly ladies reclining in armchairs each with one leg held straight up in the air. They appeared to be in great distress, though he could not imagine what was the matter with them. Perhaps they had been seized with cramp. If only he could do something to help! He left the window and banged loudly on the door again, hoping to attract the attention of Mrs McConkey, but this only seemed to make matters worse. From within came cries of dismay.

'There is someone at the door! Someone has come to call! Oh, do something, do something, don't just sit there! Oh, where is Mrs McConkey?'

Then at last there were footsteps: the front door opened and Mr Jamboree found himself face to face with Mrs McConkey, who looked highly displeased to see him. She opened her mouth in surprise, then shut it with a snap, trying at the same time to do likewise with the door; but Mr Jamboree had by this time become quite practised in the arts of door-to-door salesmen and stuck his foot in it, quick as a flash. Mrs McConkey swept it ineffectually with her broom, which she had forgotten to leave in the kitchen.

'Sure, it's you again,' she said crossly, 'and me just

after telling you that it's nothing we'll be wanting the day.'

'But the ladies,' said Mr Jamboree, earnestly, edging his foot a little further inside. 'The ladies! They are in very great difficulties and are requiring most immediate assistance.'

'Ladies!' snorted Mrs McConkey. 'I'll give you ladies! It's ladies you'll be getting an' all if you don't be taking your rubbishy old clobber out of me hall this minute. It's not for the likes of you I'm after polishing it half the morning.'

At this moment there came a concerted cry from the sitting-room and Mrs McConkey, realizing at last that

something was amiss, left Mr Jamboree and went to investigate. Opening the sitting-room door she gave a shriek.

'Lord bless us and save us!' she cried, 'will you be taking a look at this. What in the name of goodness do the pair of ye's think ye're doing? Lolling about like a couple o' drunks and displaying your garters to all and sundry! Mercy on us, suppose that encyclopedia fellow should have caught a glimpse of you!'

With this she caught Miss May by the arms and tried to pull her up into a sitting position, but it was useless; she was far too heavy. She just slid down again, further than before.

'The slippers, woman!' Miss Beatrice kept saying. 'Take them off! Can't you see it's the slippers?'

Mrs McConkey abandoned the top end of Great Aunt May and turned her attention to the feet. Mr Jamboree, overcome with curiosity, peeped round the door.

'Perhaps I may be of assistance, if the ladies are permitting,' he said, bowing politely. 'If you are holding the limb, madam,' he said to Mrs McConkey, who rather liked being called madam, 'I am with all speed removing the slipper.'

There were indignant cries of protest from the armchairs, but as it was clearly a case of necessity, Mr Jamboree and Mrs McConkey persevered, and in a few minutes the slippers were removed and Miss Beatrice and Miss May were once more the right way up with their feet set squarely on the hearth-rug. Though slightly tousled they quickly recovered their dignity, demanding in haughty tones the identity of their rescuer.

'Mr Jamboree, madam, at your service,' he

announced, smiling his best salesman's smile. 'I am just passing when I am hearing cries of distress, and am most pleased to have been of assistance. May I, since I am now here in your beautiful home, show you my very wide range of useful articles which I am having for sale, or, should you prefer, I am most happy to be exchanging for any article you are wishing to dispose of. Footwear, for example?'

'*Footwear*?' echoed the Great Aunts, together. 'Why should we wish to dispose of our *footwear*?'

'Any *old* footwear, madam,' said Mr Jamboree, nervously. 'Wellington boots, sandals –'

'We do not wear Wellington boots,' said Miss Beatrice.

'Nor sandals,' said Miss May.

'– gentlemen's slippers –'

'Nor gentlemen's slippers, either,' said Miss Beatrice. 'There are no gentlemen in this house. Mrs McConkey, will you show the man out. And close the door, please. There is quite a draught.'

'But madam – but madam –' cried Mr Jamboree desperately, as Mrs McConkey bundled him out into the hall. All his hopes were quite dashed by this unexpected turn of events. He had been so close to success, the slippers had been almost within his grasp, when all of a sudden they were whisked away . . .

'Wait!' came a voice from the sitting-room, just as he was being hustled into the street. 'Wait a minute! Bring the man back here, Mrs McConkey!'

Mrs McConkey turned her eyes to heaven, clicked her tongue and, jerking her head in the direction of the voice, conducted Mr Jamboree back down the hall again. His hopes began to rise as suddenly as they had fallen.

'We have an idea,' said Miss May, when they were once more gathered in the sitting-room. 'Haven't we, Beatrice?'

Miss Beatrice nodded without speaking.

'We thought,' continued Miss May, glancing apprehensively at her sister, 'we thought that perhaps after all we might have something to sell, or rather, exchange, that is if you have anything suitable.'

'Oh, yes, certainly madam,' said Mr Jamboree, smiling his beautiful flashing smile and starting to undo the suitcase. 'I am indeed having a very wide range of household articles, please permit me to show you –'

'Thank you, no,' interrupted Miss Beatrice. 'That will not be necessary. We have already decided. We will exchange this pair of slippers for that object there. That thing,' and she nodded briefly in the direction of the hatstand.

'Oh, certainly madam, certainly madam, with the greatest possible pleasure I am most certainly willing to be exchanging this humble hatstand for your beautiful slippers. Allow me to wrap it for you. Not at all, not at all, certainly, certainly, with pleasure madam, good-day, madam, good-day, good-day . . .' and bowing and scraping and picking up his belongings Mr Jamboree made his joyful and triumphant departure.

chapter 11

How Mr Jamboree Enjoyed a Quiet Half-Hour

As he turned away from the front door a feeling of the most exquisite relief filled Mr Jamboree to overflowing. Now he would have to face no Immediate Destruction; no starving rats, no dripping taps, no cauldrons full of boiling oil awaited him. He had found the slippers! He was saved.

And in addition, he had sold to those two formidable old ladies what must have been quite the most unsellable object in the world. Altogether he felt very pleased with himself.

It was a lovely afternoon, and as the Chinawoman was not expecting him till sunset which was still quite two hours away, he decided to go and sit for a while in the Cathedral Close and enjoy the good fresh air. He walked along slowly until he came to a bench beneath one of the chestnut trees; it was already occupied by an elderly gentleman with a pipe, but the suitcase was heavy and he did not wish to go any further.

'I trust I am not inconveniencing you, sir, by sitting down upon this bench beside you?' he said politely. 'To tell the truth, I am having a somewhat tiring day.'

'Not in the least, not in the least, perfectly all right, my dear fellow,' said the old gentleman vacantly, shifting along the seat to make room for him. 'Bicycle's not in your way, I hope?'

Mr Jamboree sat down thankfully. It was pleasant to

rest after such an exhausting and worrying day, and in his life there was little time for idleness. From dawn to dusk he was at the beck and call of the Chinawoman, who had brought him from India when he was twelve years old, and for whom he was obliged to work like a slave in order to repay her for this kindness, and also for the expense of the fare.

He often dreamed of the day when he would be a free man, no longer having to work in that dark and stuffy little shop where the sun never shone and the air never moved. When he was free he would live in the open air always: he would go into business with his friend in the market. Together they would stand beneath the beautiful painted sign of the Taj Mahal Bazaar, selling real Indian things, scarves and veils of bright gossamer silk, necklaces and earrings and bangles such as he remembered seeing in the bazaars in his far-off boyhood days. But many years of servitude must pass before he would have a chance to do this.

On the bench beside him the old gentleman puffed away at his pipe, his eyes gazing into the far blue distance beyond the Cathedral. He seemed unaware of Mr Jamboree's presence. And Mr Jamboree, coming back to earth, began to think of the slippers and of how extraordinary it was that he had not known they were in the box.

He opened the suitcase and took them out; he examined them carefully, turning them over in his hand, noticing the writing on the sole, but the long curving strokes, the dots and squiggles, were as meaningless to him as they had been to Martha and Mr Teago.

He had a sudden desire to put them on. Turning a

little away from his companion, he bent down and unlaced his tight, uncomfortable shoes.

'Bless my soul!' exclaimed Mr Teago, as the Cathedral clock struck the half-hour. 'Half past already! The evenings are drawing out wonderfully.' He knocked his pipe out on the edge of the seat and was looking round for his hat and his gloves when something caught his eye.

'Good Heavens!' he exclaimed. 'The fellow's gone off and left his bag behind! Open, too. And his *shoes*! What a singular chap! Better inform the police, I suppose.'

He put Mr Jamboree's shoes into the suitcase and closed it for him, in case anything should be stolen, then he set off across the Close in search of a policeman.

chapter 12

The Unusual Behaviour of Mr Teago's Bees

'Did you manage to get the slippers back?' Martha asked Mr Teago the next morning. He was sitting on Diddlecombe Junction looking rather down in the dumps. He shook his head sadly.

'No,' he said. 'I didn't. They wouldn't give them to me. They wouldn't even tell me where they were, but said they'd bought me another present instead, and never wished to hear them mentioned again. The fact is,' he said, taking a deep puff at his pipe, 'I'm afraid they've done something awful to them . . .'

'I don't suppose so,' said Martha. 'I expect they've just locked them up somewhere. They're always locking things up. What's the present?'

'Come,' said Mr Teago gloomily, 'I'll show you.'

He led the way down the garden path to the back door. 'There,' he said, opening it.

'What *is* it?' asked Martha. Half-hidden behind the scullery door stood a very tall object partly wrapped in brown paper. Curling wooden arms emerged from the top.

'Help me out with it, then we can look at it properly,' said Mr Teago.

They tipped it up and carried it with some difficulty through the narrow door and into the garden, where they set it upright on the gravel path.

'I still don't know what it is,' said Martha. 'Oh, wait! There's a label.' And she read out:

> 'The Patent Adjustable,
> Stainless, unrustable,
> Guaranteed Custom-designed,
> Folding, Extendable,
> Lasting, Dependable
> Hat-Coat-and-Boot-Stand Combined.

'Goodness!' she said, taking a walk round it. 'Where will you put it?'

'Heaven knows,' said Mr Teago. 'It's so enormous.'

'I suppose you couldn't just tell them you didn't want it?'

'Not really,' said Mr Teago. 'I couldn't very well hurt their feelings, in spite of the slippers, and they seemed to think I would love it.' And he remembered how lyrical they had become, describing all its advantages.

> 'Now your old cricket-bat
> Can go under your hat!
> Your umbrella can drip in the tray!
> And your Wellington boots
> And your bee-keeping suits
> Can be tidied completely away!
>
> There's an ash-tray and rack
> For your pipe at the back,
> And your smoker and gauntlets and veil
> Can all hang on the hooks!
> And the gardening books
> You can stack on the walking-stick rail!

There's a boot-brush and scraper!
A bin for waste-paper!
A place for your hair-brush and comb!
Such a practical, sensible,
Quite indispensable
Gift for the bachelor home!'

Useless to point out that he only had one hat, besides his bee-hat: that he always scraped his boots on the door-step: and that his pipe and his cricket-bat and every-thing else were quite all right on the luggage-rack where they had always been. And if he did manage to get it into his carriage there wouldn't be any room for him, unless of course it was folded up, in which case it was no use for anything.

'Well, we'd better take it up, anyway,' said Martha. 'We can't very well leave it here.'

So Mr Teago took the bottom and Martha the top, which was lighter, and together they staggered up the garden path till they came to the railway-carriage.

'What *are* we to do with it?' sighed Mr Teago. 'It'll never go in. Never.' He sat down on the seat, looking very depressed.

'I know what we *could* do with it,' said Martha, after a lot of thought. 'It'd make a lovely perch for the birds!'

'What a splendid idea!' said Mr Teago, brightening. 'What a capital plan! Do you think your Aunts will object?'

'I expect so,' said Martha. 'They usually do. But if it won't go in, it won't go in, will it?'

Mr Teago agreed that it would not. He stood up and walked round the Hat-Coat-and-Boot-Stand, consider-ing its possibilities.

'We could make a swing for them here,' he said,

'between the pegs, and one or two nesting-boxes here, and there are plenty of hooks for coconuts and that sort of thing.'

'And they can drink out of that tin tray thing at the bottom,' said Martha. 'It'll make a lovely little pond.'

'It'll be a perfect bird-paradise!' said Mr Teago.

They set to, happily and busily collecting things they thought the birds would appreciate and fixing them on to the hatstand. Mr Teago tied a bunch of evergreen leaves to the knob on the top to make them feel more at home, and Martha ran down to the kitchen to beg some crumbs and bacon-rind from Mrs McConkey.

'At this time of year!' said Mrs McConkey. 'It'd be a miserable old class of a bird, I'm thinking, that couldn't be finding a bite to eat in the month o' May, with all them fine young peas and the worms there is in the garden! But it'll give the poor man something to do, no doubt, and take his mind off his slippers.' So, grumbling away, she found some crusts and scraps of fat and gave them to Martha in a paper bag.

Mr Teago was sitting on the seat and, as Martha approached, he held up one hand for silence. He was gazing intently at the beehives.

'What's the matter?' whispered Martha.

'*Primrose*,' whispered Mr Teago, still looking at the hives as if he couldn't believe his eyes. 'Quite extraordinary! *Primrose – are – about – to – swarm…*!'

And as he spoke Martha became aware of a great humming and thrumming that filled the air, and she saw that dozens of bees were flying around very fast, in a great state of excitement, just like people preparing for a journey. Then, suddenly, more and more of them, hundreds upon hundreds, began to pour out of the hive until the air was quite filled with them. As she watched, they gathered together into an almost solid mass and rose slowly into the air above her head.

For a moment Mr Teago seemed quite paralysed with amazement, and remained sitting on Diddlecombe Junction muttering 'Astonishing! Incredible! So early …' Then, smiting himself suddenly on the head, he jumped up and rushed into the carriage; a moment later he emerged, laden with bee-paraphernalia, and set off at a smart trot down the garden path.

'Hurry! Hurry!' he called to Martha, putting his hat on as he went. 'We shall lose them if we don't make haste! Here, you take the tray.'

Out of the garden, down the alley, across the road rushed Mr Teago, heedless of bicycle bells and motorcar horns. They came to the High Street with its everlasting traffic-jam like some kind of glacier on wheels, and still they ran, leaving a trail of startled passers-by, some merely indignant, others quite badly injured.

'*So* sorry! *So* sorry!' called Martha over her shoulder, not daring to stop for fear of losing Mr Teago as well as the swarm. Through the archway they ran, and past the Butter-Cross, and still the bees travelled before them like the column of smoke before the Israelites, and by this time Martha was very much out of breath; but at last they came to the iron posts and, as they passed into the Close, Mr Teago's breakneck speed slackened.

'There they – puff – are!' he said; and, too much out of breath to say any more, he put the straw skep down on the ground and pointed overhead to where, high up in the branches of an enormous ash tree, could be seen the great solid mass of bees, so densely packed that they looked like a huge over-ripe pear about to drop.

'Can't *think* – puff, puff – what can have made them – puff – so early,' said Mr Teago. 'Extraordinary!'

'What's that thing right up in the branches, above them?' asked Martha, squinting up into the tree. 'Right at the top, see? It looks like a scarecrow or something . . .'

chapter 13

The Catching of the Swarm

'Over here,' said Mr Teago, taking the straw skep away from Martha and setting it down in a different place. 'That's better. Uphill, you see. They always go uphill.'

Having recovered his breath he was now very busy trying to recover his bees, and had spread a large sheet on the ground directly under the swarm. 'Now', he said, 'the tin tray.'

Martha passed it to him and, much to her embarrassment, he began to beat upon it, setting up a frightful din. Quite a few spectators had gathered by this time, but Mr Teago banged away oblivious of them all, beseeching his bees to come down.

'Come, my pretties! Come, my beauties! Best bees in the whole of England! Come to Uncle Teago, that's the style!' Bang, bang, crash-crash-bang.

At last, evidently in answer to Mr Teago's pleading, they came. Slowly they seemed to drop from the branch, to become a looser mass, with the ones on the edge of the great conglomeration buzzing round as if trying to see what was going on in the middle. Down and down they fell, while Mr Teago banged and cajoled, and at last in their countless thousands they settled in a wavering, living heap upon the sheet.

Sounds of wonderment came from the bystanders as they shuffled backwards to a safer distance.

'It's like magic!' said Martha.

'Now,' said Mr Teago, 'up you go, my lovelies! Up into the skep, that's the ticket! No dawdling, please. Come along now, come along now, in you go!' and obediently the bees began to crawl up the sheet, at first in ones and twos and then more and more of them, up, up into the mouth of the straw hive.

'There she goes! There goes the queen! Did you see her, Martha? They'll be all right now the queen's gone in. They'll all follow the queen.'

'Have they all come down?' asked Martha, peering up into the branches. 'Look, Mr Teago, what *is* that thing up there?'

Reluctantly Mr Teago took his eyes away from his bees, who were now crawling up the white cotton hill in a steady stream, like a crowd at a football match.

'A kite,' he said briefly, glancing upwards. 'Must have blown there.'

'But it's got arms,' said Martha. 'And legs. I never saw a kite with arms and legs. It looks much more like a scarecrow.'

'It's got a tail, too,' said Mr Teago, taking another look, 'and I never heard of a scarecrow having a tail. Besides, how could it have got there? Scarecrows don't fly.' And he turned his attention back to the bees.

Martha had to admit that scarecrows did not usually fly, but still she was not satisfied with Mr Teago's explanation: it simply did not look like a kite. For one thing, kites are brightly coloured, not black . . . She bent over and looked at it from an upside-down point of view, and suddenly let out a cry of amazement:

'Mr Teago! It's *not* a scarecrow!'

'I know, my dear. That's just what I was saying.'

'Yes, but it's not a kite either. We were both wrong. It's – it's *Mr Jamboree!*'

Mr Teago stood up and removed his bee-veil and his bee-hat and screwed up his eyes, but he could not really see what the object was that was stuck in the branches. It was very high up and the sun was dazzling. He shook his head in disbelief.

'But it *is*! It *is*! I know it's him!' insisted Martha, and, cupping her hands to her mouth she shouted up into the tree: 'Mr Jamboree! Mr Jamboreeeeeeeee!'

In answer there came a faint sound from the tree-top, harsh and thin as the cry of a starling. 'Yes, yes, it is I, J. Jamboree. I am sticking in these branches. Please be summoning the Fire Brigade with all speed.'

'Good Heavens!' exclaimed Mr Teago: 'I do believe it's the fellow with the suitcase who was sitting beside me on the bench yesterday afternoon. What an extraordinary coincidence. And how in the world did he manage to get up there? My dear sir,' he shouted, cupping his hands to his mouth, 'what a remarkable feat!'

'No, no!' came Mr Jamboree's voice faintly out of the tree-top. 'It is not my feet: rather it is the slippers that are being remarkable. Oh, do please be so good as to send at once for the Fire Brigade ...' His voice tailed away pathetically.

'Did he say *slippers*?' said Martha. 'That means – that means that it must have been *him*! Now I understand it all! He must have got the slippers back from the Great Aunts, and sold them the hatstand! And then he must have put the slippers on while he was sitting beside you, and that's why he left his suitcase behind! He just floated up into the tree and got stuck in the branches! Well, it jolly well serves him right.'

'All the same,' said Mr Teago, 'perhaps we should try to get him down. The poor chap must be dashed

70

uncomfortable. We can't very well just leave him there.'

Martha considered. 'Perhaps you're right,' she said at last. 'But I don't think we should get the fire engine. It would upset the bees, and anyway it wouldn't be allowed in the Close. I'll climb up and take the slippers off and then he'll be able to come down by himself.'

Mr Teago was not sure that he ought to allow Martha to climb such a very high tree, but there really seemed no other way of rescuing the unfortunate Jamboree, and eventually he agreed. He hoisted her up on to the lowest branch.

'Hold on, sir! Hold on!' he shouted to Mr Jamboree. 'We'll have you down in a jiffy. Chin up!'

Martha began to climb, while Mr Teago watched her from below with mounting anxiety.

'Take care, Martha, do take care!' he called. 'Oh dear, I don't like to think what your Aunts would say. Oh dear, oh dear...'

chapter 14

How Martha Vanished Into Space

Ten minutes later Mr Jamboree, somewhat shaken, stood once more on solid ground.

'Many many thanks,' he said, bowing to Mr Teago. He brushed the leaves and twigs from his coat and began to rewind the long white tail of his turban.

'Ah, now I see why I mistook you for a kite,' said Mr Teago thoughtfully, stroking his chin. 'I must apologize. It was Martha, of course, who recognized you. Which reminds me: she ought to be down by now. I wonder what's happened. Mar-tha!'

'I'm STUCK!' came Martha's voice from the top of the tree. 'Mr Jamboree has broken all the branches!'

'It is true,' said Mr Jamboree. 'But truly I could not help it. When the young lady kindly pulled the slippers off I just came crashing down until, fortunately, I am falling across that large bough above your head. Otherwise, no doubt, I should have been killed. But I am sorry about the branches. Perhaps we had better be sending at once for the Fire Brig—'

'No, sir, we can not,' said Mr Teago firmly, cutting him short. 'I cannot have my bees disturbed any more. We shall have to climb up ourselves and rescue her.'

'But how is that being possible?' asked Mr Jamboree. 'With no branches?'

'Oh dear, oh dear,' said Mr Teago. 'You are quite

right. Then I am afraid there is only one thing for it: she will have to come down by slippers.'

'By slippers?'

Mr Teago nodded. 'It is the only way. Though I must confess I do not like to *think* what her Aunts would say. Oh, my poor little Martha...'

Martha, swaying about in the branches overhead, had come to the same conclusion as Mr Teago, and she did not feel very happy about it either. With a feeling of resignation she kicked off her sandals and watched them fall and fall till they hit the ground. Perhaps that was what would happen to her, if the slippers did not work.

'We-will-catch-you-in-the-sheet!' came Mr Teago's voice from far below; and looking down through the few remaining branches Martha could see the two little figures, tiny as dolls, holding a white square as big as a pocket handkerchief.

'When you're ready!' cried Mr Teago.

But Martha did not feel at all ready; she was not sure that she ever would. It was one thing to float round the kitchen table in Mr Teago's slippers, but quite another to cast yourself out of the topmost twigs of an enormous tree trusting in a little bit of very old and possibly worn-out magic to keep you from crashing to the ground. She looked again at the minute white sheet and shuddered slightly. Then she took a deep breath to give herself courage and, holding tightly to the tree with one arm, wriggled and squiggled until she finally managed to get both her feet into the slippers...

'Oh, Martha, Martha,' said Mr Teago miserably, as he stood with Mr Jamboree holding out the white square of cotton that was to save her life; 'Oh, do come down safely! Oh dear, oh dear!'

For what seemed hours they stared up into the tree,
waiting for the moment when she would come sailing,
or perhaps plummeting down, and the strain grew
almost unbearable.

'There she is going!' cried Mr Jamboree suddenly.
'There! There!'

And Mr Teago, following the direction of Mr Jamboree's arm, was astonished to behold a tiny figure go
shooting up out of the tree-top like an untied balloon,
diving and swooping and looping the loop, swifter than
the eye could follow. In less than half a minute she had
vanished.

Horror-stricken, Mr Teago and Mr Jamboree continued to stare at the spot in the sky where they had last seen her, their mouths agape, their hands still clutching the sheet.

'This is terrible,' said Mr Teago at last, leaning weakly against the tree. 'Terrible. I ought to have known that they would go up, not down.'

'Sir,' said Mr Jamboree, 'do not blame yourself. It is my fault. My fault entirely. If it had not been for me it would not have happened at all. Perhaps, after all, it would have been better to have had the Fire Brigade. I am offering heart-felt apologies.'

Mr Teago did not answer. All he could think of was that he had sent Martha whizzing off into space, even, perhaps, to her death, and that he would never, never see her again. He felt numb with desolation. Taking the corners of the sheet from Mr Jamboree he began automatically to fold it.

'I shall have to tell them,' he muttered. 'Better do it straight away, I suppose.' With an effort he turned to Mr Jamboree. 'Give me a hand, would you, there's a good fellow. A bit awkward on one's own...'

They set off across the Close. Mr Teago went in front with the skep, surrounded by a cloud of bees; behind him Mr Jamboree padded along in his socks, carrying everything else. Mr Teago sought comfort from his bees, talking to them as he went:

'Oh bees, bees, what am I to do? I should never have allowed it, and now I must tell the Great Aunts, and how in the world am I going to break it to them? How can a fellow say, "Oh excuse me, by the bye, I'm very sorry to tell you that I've just accidentally sent your great niece into orbit. Just floated off, she did. Very fast. Awfully sorry ..."? I dare say it doesn't

sound all that terrible to you bees, who are quite
accustomed to flying about, but I assure you it's a very
different matter for human beings. Very different
indeed. Oh dear, oh dear, oh dear . . .'

Behind him, Mr Jamboree broke into a trot.

'I should be most obliged to you, sir,' he began, in an
aggrieved tone of voice, 'if you would not be walking
quite so exceptionally fast. I am merely in my socks as I
am not having any shoes, and the gravel is painful to be
saying the least. Also this bag is very heavy and this tin
tray very awkward. I am not understanding why it is
necessary to be carrying a tin tray at all, if I may say so.
In addition –' and here his voice broke into a sob '– I am
nearly dying with hunger!'

But Mr Teago was much too concerned with his own
thought to pay any attention to poor Mr Jamboree
who, hobbling and limping, followed as closely upon
his flying heels as he was able, until at last they
reached the alley.

Mr Teago set the straw skep carefully down and
pressed the latch of the door with trembling fingers.

chapter 15

How Martha Came Back to Earth

Mr Teago, feeling sick with misery, opened the garden door and beheld to his surprise the three figures of Miss Beatrice, Miss May and Mrs McConkey standing in a row with their backs towards him, looking at something on the ground. Miss May poked it with the toe of her shoe, and with a surge of horror Mr Teago saw that it was Martha.

'No, no!' he murmured faintly, immediately fearing the worst. He clapped his hand to his eyes and leaned against the doorpost. 'She can't be . . . She can't be . . .'

'She *can't* be allowed to lie about in the garden all day!' came Great Aunt Beatrice's strident tones. 'Fine weather or no fine weather! She's becoming thoroughly idle!'

'Thoroughly!' agreed Great Aunt May. 'The idea! Lazing about in the day-time!'

'It's not lazing about she is at all,' said Mrs McConkey, suddenly dropping to her knees beside Martha's prostrate form. 'Did you not see her come hurtling out of the sky? It's knocked out cold she is, and a mercy she's not kilt dead!'

'Tree-climbing again, I suppose,' said Great Aunt May. 'Ah, well, she's been told and told.'

'Serves her perfectly right,' said Great Aunt Beatrice. 'It will do her good.'

'It's not after climbing trees she is,' said Mrs

McConkey, 'nor roofs, nor chimney-pots nor walls. It's them rubbishy old slippers of Mr Teago's that's the cause of all the trouble.'

'Nonsense, woman! She has nothing on her feet but her stockings.'

'And wouldn't that be just the very reason that she crashed?' demanded Mrs McConkey. 'If they was still on her feet it's gallivanting up in the sky she'd be, not lying here in the spring greens, knocked out of her senses.'

'In any case,' said Great Aunt May, 'we have got rid of the wretched things, so they could not be the cause of the trouble, could they?'

At this moment Martha stirred and opened her eyes. 'Ooh, my head!' she said, and closed them again. Mr Teago rushed across the lawn.

'Oh, Martha, Martha! Are you all right? Oh, tell me you're all right!' He knelt stiffly down beside her.

'I think I am,' said Martha, opening her eyes again. 'Except for my head. Feel. There's a huge bump. What am I doing here, in your cabbages?'

Mr Teago felt so overcome with relief that he could not speak. She was all right! Perhaps a little concussed, but that was all! She was not dead, or lost in space, or even badly injured, but lying in her own garden in a nice soft bed of cabbages.

'How did I get here?' she asked, looking round. 'I can't remember ... And Mr Jamboree! What are you doing here?'

The Great Aunts turned round at the mention of Mr Jamboree's name. He wriggled under their searing gaze like a caterpillar sprayed with Flit, and tried vainly to hide one shoe-less foot behind the other.

'And what is *that* I see in the Lonicera?' asked Great Aunt Beatrice, whose eyes were now searching the garden as if expecting to discover a Jamboree lurking behind every bush. She directed a ferocious glance towards the hedge.

'A slipper! A slipper!' cried Mr Jamboree, darting past the little group and setting off across the flower-bed in the direction indicated by Miss Beatrice's chin. 'Three cheers! Hooray! Perhaps after all I shall be escaping Total Destruction.'

But Mrs McConkey was too quick for him. 'No you don't!' she cried, taking a short cut behind the bean-poles and fishing it out of the hedge with the washing-tongs which she happened to be carrying. 'It's enough trouble we've had with them already,' she cried, 'and it's putting an end to them I am this minute. Sure, they're enough to drive a Christian body to his grave, so they are!'

'I fancy I see the other one in the Plantagenista,' said

Great Aunt May, who was rather proud of her Latin names.

'What are you doing with them?' asked Martha, getting unsteadily to her feet. 'Oh *no*, Mrs McConkey! Oh, stop! *Please* stop!'

'Oh, indeed, do not do anything rash,' joined in Mr Jamboree, setting off in pursuit of Mrs McConkey. 'I am to return them to my mistress immediately, otherwise I am facing the most terribly consequences … Hungry rats … burning oil … Oh, please!'

But Mrs McConkey paid no heed to him. She stumped away to the corner of the garden, collecting the second slipper on the way and threw them both on to the burning rubbish incinerator. 'There!' she said, triumphantly, swishing one hand against the other; 'and it's no more trouble we'll be having from *them*, I'm hoping. Flibberty-gibberty heathenish things.'

Martha and Mr Teago watched, aghast, waiting for the slippers to burst into flames; Martha would have rescued them from the fire had not Mr Teago held her firmly by the wrist for fear of her being burned. Mr Jamboree sat down on a rhubarb-pot and buried his head in his hands.

But, strange to say, the slippers did not burst into flames at all. For a few moments they just hoved above the fire, rising and falling gently in the heat, and then all of a sudden they whirled upwards, twisting and turning in the spiral of smoke like two little birds. In the garden below everybody watched, astounded, as they drifted higher and higher above the roof-tops until finally they were lost to sight.

'Good Riddance,' said Great Aunt Beatrice.

'To Bad Rubbish,' said Great Aunt May.

There was silence.

At least, nobody spoke: though there was still the faraway hum of the city and the summer-song of birds and the buzzing of bees.

'Bees!' exclaimed Mr Teago suddenly. 'Good heavens! I had quite forgotten them. They are still in the alley.'

He turned and opened the door in the wall, and as he did so the others, standing in the garden, heard him gasp in surprise. Framed in the doorway stood the Chinawoman.

chapter 16

How Madame Wu Let Off Some Firecrackers

When, the evening before, sunset had come, and with it no sign of the slippers or Mr Jamboree, Madame Wu knew that her threats had failed and that she would have to try to find them herself; and so it was that, with the aid of some ancient Chinese sorcery, she did at last succeed in tracking them down.

First she had had to consult at length the thirteen scrolls of the Chinese calendar, which gave the most auspicious dates for Dying, Marrying, Being Born and Declaring War, as well as for less important things, such as Wreaking Vengeance and Finding Treasure. By a lucky chance the following day was forecast as being ideal for these last two undertakings, and it was with a feeling of hope that she had rolled up the calendar and gone to bed.

Early the next morning she had sat down at the little lacquer table with a map of the town spread out upon it; above it, suspended from the middle finger of her left hand, a silver arrowhead swung on a silken thread. The Chinawoman watched it intently as it moved across the town, now swinging slowly over the Town Hall, now whirling round the Hospital. Patiently she waited for the moment when it would begin to circle more and more slowly, finally to stop above the place where, she knew, she would find the slippers . . .

And now, as she stood in the doorway of Number

Eleven, she knew that the arrow had not failed her: that
here she would find her treasure. For a full minute she
surveyed the scene in the garden, her narrow black eyes
moving from Great Aunt to Great Aunt, to the defiant
figure of Mrs McConkey, to Mr Teago who was still
holding on to Martha, to the horrified figure of Mr
Jamboree quaking on the rhubarb-pot. Suddenly he
flung himself at her feet and began to jabber inco-
herently:

'Truly, truly, mistress, I am trying to stop her! I am
wishing to return them to you by sunset as we are
arranging, and would have done so but for an unfortunate incident which is detaining me unavoidably. Oh,
mercy, mercy, mistress! I am beseeching you, do not do
anything awful! I am indeed trying very very hard and I
am regretting most deeply that the slippers are still
escaping me –'

'Silence!'

Mr Jamboree stopped talking as everybody turned towards the small figure of Madame Wu. She made a sudden movement, flinging wide her arms and instantly the whole place was filled with a terrible battery of noise as if a hundred gnomes were letting off toy pistols in every corner of the garden. Mr Jamboree leapt on top of his rhubarb-pot and Martha buried her head in Mr Teago's stomach.

'It's all right,' said Mr Teago, in rather a shaky voice. 'It's only firecrackers. They're very keen on them in China.'

The toy pistols had stopped, but now the whole place became filled with smoke so that you could hardly see across the garden. It was swirling so thickly round Mr Jamboree that he was almost invisible, though they could hear him coughing dreadfully; the Chinawoman herself had quite disappeared from view. The breeze was wafting it all over the place, and now Mrs McConkey and the Great Aunts were only visible in parts. Prudently Martha and Mr Teago moved up-wind, into the shelter of the garden wall. At last, however, the smoke began to clear.

Suddenly Martha tugged Mr Teago's sleeve. 'Look!' she whispered. 'Look at Mr Jamboree! Whatever's happening to him? He's sort of – sort of *changing*!'

In horrified fascination they watched, hardly able to believe their eyes as, slowly, the dark figure of Mr Jamboree seemed to alter, becoming somehow blacker and blacker . . . and smaller . . . until he was hardly any larger than . . .

'A mynah bird!' breathed Mr Teago incredulously. 'I do declare – she's *turned him into a mynah bird* before our very eyes! Incredible!'

I'm dreaming, thought Martha. I must be. People don't just turn into mynah birds like that, in the middle of the day! Of course it's a dream; all of it; waking up in the cabbage-bed and everything ... And being up in that huge great tree, and wasn't I flying? Whirling through the sky like a rocket, right over the Cathedral, and all the saints and the gargoyles on the roof were looking at me! And then I remember falling and falling and falling ...

'Look!' said Mr Teago, clutching her arm in a very undreamlike fashion, 'Martha! Look at the China-woman! Something's happened to *her*, *too*!'

And so it was. Just as Mr Jamboree had grown smaller and blacker, so was the Chinawoman growing smaller and yellower, and somehow fluffier ... and silkier ... 'Great Scot!' said Mr Teago, almost too amazed to utter. 'I'm dashed if she isn't changing into a – into a silky! A silky bantam, you know. Look at her trousers!'

It was quite true: the slim silk trousers under Madame Wu's tunic were growing featherier and feath-erier, and her *feet*! Something most peculiar was happening to her feet ... In no time at all she was a bantam.

'*Goodness*!' said Martha, still whispering. 'Do you think she meant to?'

'I don't know,' said Mr Teago, whispering back. 'Perhaps she can't stop.'

'D'you think she's going to change us, too? I wonder what we'll become?'

'I don't very much want to become anything,' said Mr Teago. 'I'd rather stay as I am, rheumatism and all!'

At last all the smoke disappeared and Martha and

Mr Teago found themselves alone in the garden, except for Mr Jamboree and the Chinawoman, or rather, what used to be Mr Jamboree and the Chinawoman. The Great Aunts had evidently gone indoors, for there was nobody on the lawn but two fat pigeons.

'Pigeons!' said Martha suddenly, her eyes round with wonder. 'You don't think – they *couldn't* be – *could* they?'

Mr Teago looked more closely at the pigeons: there was indeed a certain look about them – a kind of haughty air – which seemed familiar, though of course they were much smaller and rounder and greyer ...

He nodded. 'I'm afraid so.'

'It must have been that smoke,' said Martha. 'It blew everywhere. Do you think *we* will change, too? I'd rather like to be a swallow, I think ... Where's Mrs McConkey?'

'I don't know,' said Mr Teago, looking round. 'I don't know where she is. But I don't remember ever seeing that brown hen before!'

'Oh, goodness!' said Martha; and all of a sudden she felt as if she didn't know whether to laugh or cry, it was all so very peculiar.

Martha and Mr Teago spent the rest of the afternoon making homes for everyone to live in. They fixed a wooden box on to one end of Mr Teago's carriage for the Great Aunts, with two front doors and a partition inside, in case of disagreements. Mrs McConkey, it was decided, should share the old chicken-coop with Madame Wu. Mr Jamboree had a nice house to himself, made from a little wooden barrel with a hole cut in the side for an entrance and two perches inside. In silence he allowed himself to be picked up and placed

87

upon the doorstep. Martha watched eagerly to see how he would like his new home, but he seemed too dazed by his recent experience to do anything but stand there, blinking his sad yellow eyes.

'Perhaps if we were to leave him for a while ...' suggested Mr Teago. 'After all, it must have been a bit of a shock for the poor fellow.'

So they left him, and turned their attention to Madame Wu who was energetically scratching up the pinks that edged the rose-bed. She seemed to have decided to remain.

'Excuse me, madam,' said Mr Teago, uncertain how to address her. 'Shoo!'

'We could shut her up in the chicken-coop,' said Martha.

This, however, proved impossible. Madame Wu could not be caught. However swiftly they pounced upon her, however cunningly they enticed her into corners, she always managed to elude them, slipping sideways out of their grasp and giving them a most disdainful look. In the end they gave it up.

'She'll just have to roost in the tree,' said Mr Teago.

He sat down upon Diddlecombe Junction and lit his pipe while Martha went into the carriage and put the kettle on the little gas stove. It had been a tiring afternoon.

It was while they were drinking their tea that they were suddenly startled by a voice close beside them: 'Good morning, ladies! Good morning, ladies! Can I interest you in my very wide range of household articles? Good morning!'

Mr Jamboree had found his voice.

chapter 17

How Martha Went to Stay with Mr Teago

That night Mr Teago put Martha to bed in his own bedroom, while he slept in the sitting-room, which was, in fact, very much the same as the bedroom, except that smoking was permitted. The house, with nobody in it but Martha, had seemed somehow very large and dark and full of noises, and she had felt much happier in Mr Teago's carriage.

When she awoke the next morning she lay for a long time noticing all the strange and interesting things about her: the way the ceiling curved at the edges instead of sloping, as hers did, under the eaves; and the way the luggage-rack stretched like a sort of giant cob-web right across the carriage. The windows all had little blinds with fringes and tassels and on the panes were mysterious writings:

There was a notice on the door, too, warning her that she was forbidden to lean out of the window, above which she could see the communication cord with its even more alarming message:

PENALTY FOR
IMPROPER USE
£5

All in all, it seemed safer to stay in bed, and as she was in no hurry to get up she turned over on her side in the narrow little bunk and, propping her head on one hand, examined in detail the nice views of Porchester Castle and Bognor Regis.

Meanwhile, Mr Teago, having dressed himself and put the kettle on, had stepped outside to see how everyone had slept.

'You arrrrre – so – stupid,' said Great Aunt Beatrice (that is, the pigeon that used to be Great Aunt Beatrice) as he passed the dovecote; and the pigeon that used to be Great Aunt May echoed, 'You arrrrre – so – stupid!'

'Good morning, my dears,' answered Mr Teago, not in the least put out, for he knew the poor things could not help it: that is what pigeons always say. He moved on to the chicken-coop and lifted up the middle bar.

'Cluck-cluck-cluck-cluck-CLUCK-cluck!' said Mrs McConkey, with unmistakable pride; and looking inside, Mr Teago was thrilled to discover not one, but two brown eggs!

'Mrs McConkey!' he beamed; 'that's just what we wanted. Many, many thanks!'

Mr Jamboree was still sleeping and Mr Teago did not disturb him, thinking that it would be nice for the poor chap to have a 'long lie' for once – or should it be a 'long perch'? Madame Wu was already scratching up the flower-bed: politely Mr Teago shooed her away.

By the time he returned to the carriage Martha had laid the table and made some tea. Excitedly Mr Teago showed her Mrs McConkey's eggs.

'Do you think we *ought* to eat them?' asked Martha doubtfully. Somehow it didn't seem right.

'Of course,' said Mr Teago. 'That's what she laid them for. Specially. I could tell.'

So they boiled them tenderly, and ate them with reverence, and they were delicious.

'All the same,' said Martha, wiping her mouth with the back of her hand, as there was no one to tell her not to, 'all the same, I wish she would change back again.'

Mr Teago wished so too; indeed he even found himself wishing that the Great Aunts would also change back again, for in spite of their faults he was fond of them and it seemed somehow rather dull without them. He began to feel slightly depressed.

'Was it really true about the slippers?' asked Martha.

'About them flying away, I mean? Or did I dream it?'

'It was true,' said Mr Teago. And for a moment they both sat in silence, remembering how the slippers had spiralled into the sky, weaving and twisting round each other so that as they rose they had looked just like two little multicoloured birds.

'Shall we go and give them all some breakfast?' asked Martha after a while, remembering the Great Aunts and Mrs McConkey. 'Do you think Mr Jamboree will have woken up yet?'

She spread a tablecloth on the grass outside Mr Teago's carriage and put five saucers on it, one for each bird. She put some breadcrumbs and cornflakes into Mrs McConkey's and Rice Krispies into Madame Wu's and Mr Jamboree's, knowing from Geography that Rice is the Staple Diet in India and China. She was not sure what to give the Great Aunts.

'What do pigeons eat?' she called to Mr Teago.

'Oh, young cabbages, early pears, anything, really,' said Mr Teago, ruefully. 'They're not fussy!'

'You arrrrre – so – stupid!' said both the Great Aunts together.

'Breakfast!' called Mr Teago, when all was ready; and with a great flutter and bustle Mrs McConkey and the Great Aunts arrived, followed by Madame Wu, who held herself very much aloof, choosing the saucer furthest away from the others and refusing to speak to anyone. Mr Jamboree was too nervous to join them, so Martha gave him his Rice Krispies in his own house.

When they had all finished Martha cleared away their saucers and folded up the tablecloth and was just going back into the railway carriage when something strange caught her eye.

'Mr Teago! Look! *Look* what's hanging on the hat-stand!'

'What, bless my soul!' said Mr Teago, stepping down into the garden, 'dash me if they haven't come back! They really are the most *remarkable* slippers!'

chapter 18

How the Summer Came to an End

From that day onwards throughout the long and lovely summer Mr Teago and Martha lived very happily, tending to the wants of their strange charges. Martha soon gave up laying the table properly, for she could not stop them putting their feet on the cloth – and as they always seemed to prefer everybody else's food to their own it seemed pointless to give them separate plates. Besides, it was much less trouble just to throw everything on to the grass. The Great Aunts had to be watched, for they had become extremely greedy since they turned into pigeons, and would advance upon poor little Mr Jamboree with open beaks, telling him repeatedly how stupid he was.

'Good morning, ladies!' he would say, backing away into the flower bed. Mrs McConkey, however, was very motherly towards him, protecting him with outstretched wings and scratching up worms for him with her feet.

The summer term began, but I am sorry to say that sometimes Martha did not go to school. On those days the Great Aunts would puff themselves out and say more often than ever, 'you arrrre – so – stupid!' but nobody paid them any attention. Martha would shoo them off Mr Teago's cabbages and threaten to give them no supper and they would strut away, muttering to each other.

Sometimes in the evenings, when everyone had gone to roost, Martha and Mr Teago would have Slipper Practice. In the beginning they had been very cautious about it and had only worn one slipper, keeping the other foot very firmly on the ground, and Mr Teago had tied Martha to Diddlecombe Junction for fear of her taking off. But as time went on they both got better and better at it, until they could glide and float, swoop and hover, controlling both speed and altitude without difficulty. And sometimes they would wind up Mr Teago's gramophone and, wearing one slipper each, dance to the crackly strains of 'Little Brown Jug', doing enormous hops on the count of three. Then, packing the slippers safely away in the red box, they would clamber up the steps into the railway carriage and go to bed, pleasantly exhausted.

So the days went by, peacefully and happily. Mrs McConkey continued to lay two eggs a day and occasionally they would find some belonging to Madame Wu as well, carefully hidden in some secret place, for she kept herself very much to herself. Mr Teago grew two rows of everything, one for themselves and one for the Great Aunts, who had grown extremely fat.

And then one morning there were no eggs in Mrs McConkey's chicken-coop, and Mrs McConkey herself looked decidedly off-colour. Her proud red comb drooped palely over one eye and her feathers came out in mops all over the garden. Martha ran to find Mr Teago.

'It's Mrs McConkey!' she cried. 'I think she's ill.'

'No,' said Mr Teago, after consultation with a neighbour. 'It's the Moult. She's going into the Moult.'

'Oh,' said Martha.

A few days later the same thing began to happen to the Great Aunts. Stray green and purple feathers kept falling out of their necks like hairpins from a bun, and they looked distinctly ruffled up. Mr Teago bought them a tonic, but it did no good.

'You arrrre – so – stupid!' said Great Aunt Beatrice ungratefully.

'There's something happening to all of them,' said Martha. 'Madame Wu has even stopped scratching, and Mr Jamboree has forgotten his lines. He's got them all muddled up. You listen!'

'Good morning articles!' said Mr Jamboree. 'Can I interest you in my very wide range of household ladies? Good morning! I can offer an interesting range of very wide ladies. Good morning households! Good morning –' His voice trailed away confusedly.

And then one morning he had gone. Martha and Mr Teago stood side by side looking at his empty barrel, as if by staring long enough they could bring him back.

'I suppose he's migrated,' said Mr Teago sadly. 'India, of course.'

'It's an awful long way,' said Martha. 'Will he be all right?'

Tears began to trickle down Martha's cheeks, and a cold autumny wind whistled through the michaelmas daisies. Summer was over.

'Where are the Great Aunts?' said Martha suddenly. 'They can't have gone away. Pigeons don't migrate, do they?'

'No,' said Mr Teago. 'I expect they're still asleep.'

But they weren't. The dovecot was empty too. There was not a sign of any of them. With a feeling of desperation she searched the garden for Madame Wu, but it was the same story: she also had flown.

That day was the saddest day of Martha's life, and probably of Mr Teago's too. They mooched about, hardly speaking, trying every now and then to busy themselves with some task or other, but everything seemed pointless. No need, now, to string black cotton over the brussels sprouts or silver paper on the tomatoes, for there was no Mrs McConkey, no Madame Wu, to scratch them up, no Great Aunts to eat them. No one to care for, no one to feed, no one to shoo, no one to marvel at, no one.

The day grew colder and duller and in the late afternoon when it would have been just about feeding-time on an ordinary day, Martha burst into tears.

'Oh-oh-oh,' she cried, with a great sob, 'I *wish* they'd come back!'

Mr Teago put his arm round her and led her gently

towards his carriage, and together they sat down upon Diddlecombe Junction.

'Don't cry,' he said; though if he had not been a man I think he would have been crying too. 'Please Martha, don't cry. We've still got the bees! And the honey! Come, we'll go down to the house and we'll make hot buttered toast for tea. It'll be nice and cosy, for I lit the stove this morning to air the place. Come on, cheer up!'

'All right,' said Martha, sniffing loudly and knocking the tears out of her eyes. 'I'll make the toast.'

chapter 19

How Martha and Mr Teago had Tea in the Kitchen

In the kitchen the stove was humming merrily; the kettle sang, the clock ticked, and a warm red glow shone on the hearth, welcoming them both.

'Did you put the kettle on?' asked Martha, surprised.

'Well, I must have,' said Mr Teago, 'if you didn't. I'm getting dreadfully forgetful these days.'

'So am I,' said Martha. 'I've forgotten the milk. And the bread.'

'You can't have,' said Mr Teago. 'They're both here on the dresser.'

That's funny, thought Martha. Very odd! But then, it had been an odd sort of day altogether ...

She started to make the toast, sitting on the hearth and holding the old brass toasting-fork up to the bars of the grate. She began to feel a bit happier.

'It almost like old times,' said Mr Teago. He was laying the table. 'I wonder if there are any biscuits left in the tin ... It feels quite full!'

'I thought we'd finished them long ago,' said Martha.

'Well,' said Mr Teago, 'I thought so too. I suppose it must have been another tin or something.' He began to arrange the biscuits on a plate, turning them sugar-side up so that the pictures showed. Suddenly he stopped.

'What was that?'

'I don't know!' whispered Martha. 'It sounded like – a foot-fall. There it is again!'

She reached for Mr Teago's hand and, as her fingers closed round his, the kitchen door opened with a long-drawn-out creak and who should walk in but – Mrs McConkey.

'Oh!' cried Martha, rushing towards her and flinging her arms round her neck. 'Mrs McConkey! Oh, Mrs McConkey! You've come back!' And for some reason she could not in the least understand, she burst into tears.

'Lord bless us!' said Mrs McConkey, disengaging herself and smoothing her hair. 'What in the world's come over the child? And why wouldn't I be coming back indeed?'

'We thought – sniff – we thought you'd – sniff – gone away,' said Martha, drying her eyes with her sleeve. 'Like all the others.'

'Like *what* others?' said Mrs McConkey. 'Whatever are you talking about? I'm only after taking in the mistresses' tea and you welcome me back to me own kitchen as if I'd been to America!'

'The *mistresses' tea*?' echoed Martha. 'Are they back, too?'

'Well, it's only out to the post they've been and they weren't gone more than ten minutes,' said Mrs McConkey. 'Though to be sure it's a great appetite they both have, for they're pecking away in there like a pair of pigeons.'

'*Pigeons!*'

'If you look in the bottom oven, Martha, there's a few scones over we may as well be eating ourselves. I see you found the biscuits.' She sat down in the old basket chair and began to pour out the tea. Martha and Mr Teago both found that they could not stop looking at her, so wonderful was it to have her back again, and, indeed, so extraordinary.

'Is it a smut I have on me nose or what,' said Mrs McConkey, 'that the pair of you keep staring at me as if you hadn't seen me for half a year? What's up with you?'

'Oh, nothing, nothing,' said Mr Teago hastily, looking hard at his scone.

'It's just that it's so *lovely* to see you!' said Martha.

'Will you listen to the child,' said Mrs McConkey. 'It's clean daft she's gone! Dear goodness, there goes the bell for me to fetch the tea-tray. No peace for the wicked!'

But Martha reached the door before her. 'I'll fetch it!' she cried. 'I want to see them!'

'Wait for me,' said Mr Teago, hurrying after her. 'I'll help you.'

'Well!' said Mrs McConkey, sinking back into her chair and scratching her head. There certainly was something very peculiar about them both today! In all the years she had known Martha she could not recollect one occasion on which the child had actually *wanted* to see her Great Aunts; indeed most of her life was spent in trying to avoid them, and even Mr Teago was wont to keep out of their way until supper-time. It was very strange . . .

'Come in!' sang the familiar voice of Aunt Beatrice, in response to Martha's knock, and together they stepped into the sitting-room.

For a long moment they just stood and stared at the two old ladies in their grey tweeds and lisle-thread stockings and cairngorm brooches, and a feeling of deep happiness filled them both.

'Close the door, please,' said Great Aunt May, without looking up. She was crocheting.

'There is quite a draught,' said Great Aunt Beatrice, busily knitting. 'Why, Martha! Where is Mrs McConkey? And Timothy! Why are you here at this time of day?'

'Mrs McConkey's in the kitchen,' said Martha. 'We just wanted to see you, that's all.'

'And why in the world should you want to do that?' asked Great Aunt Beatrice tartly.

'We just thought –' began Martha.

'We just felt –' began Mr Teago.

'It's just that it's so lovely to see you again!' said Martha, and to her great surprise she found that she had rushed forward and had planted a kiss on Great Aunt Beatrice's soft old cheek. And Mr Teago was kissing Great Aunt May!

It took a few moments for everyone to regain their composure. Martha had turned very pink and Mr Teago was a dusky crimson; both the Great Aunts looked slightly ruffled.

'Really!' they said together, giving their shoulders a little wriggle and smoothing their hair; 'you *are* so stupid!'

chapter 20

The Coming of Winter

With Mrs McConkey and the Great Aunts all restored to their normal shapes, life at Number Eleven also returned to normal. School began again, and Martha found that she was really rather glad to be back, for one can, after all, have too much of a good thing, even holidays, and hers had been going on for such a long time that she had missed all of Oliver Cromwell and most of South America; as for Algebra, x seemed likely to remain the Unknown Quantity for evermore. Martha had never been much good at Algebra.

The days grew shorter and shorter and soon it was dark before she got home from school. The streets were full of umbrellas and the smell of wet overcoats, and on such evenings Martha would hurry home faster than ever to the warm welcome of the old kitchen, where Mrs McConkey would be making potato-cakes for her, or cinnamon-toast, and hot cocoa to keep out the cold. She and Mr Teago and Mrs McConkey were often able to have supper together in front of the kitchen stove, for with the coming of winter the Great Aunts became increasingly busy with Talks and Meetings and Charity Galas, and were sometimes out three or four evenings a week.

But even when they were at home the evenings were still enjoyable, for the Great Aunts seemed nowadays much less fierce than they used to be. They always allowed Mr Teago to wear his slippers and never made any nasty remarks about them. Mr Teago had, in fact, learned to control them very well by this time, and could glide all the way down the garden from his railway-carriage just skimming above the wet grass, so that he arrived for supper with perfectly dry feet, even without galoshes. Sometimes, after supper, one of the Great Aunts would even play a tune on the piano, while

the other took a stately turn or two round the carpet with him. It was often quite hard for Martha to remember that they were the same Great Aunts who, only last winter, used to keep her shivering on the doorstep when she came home from school while they gave vent to their scolding tongues:

'See your new school mackintosh!'

'See your tunic, too!'

'And all the dye –'

'From your school tie –'
'– is running navy blue!'
'To think that it was new!'
'You're soaking through and through!'
'Suppose you catch pneumonia?'
'Suppose you catch the flu?'
'Or just a chill. If you are ill –'
'– We're sure to catch it too!'
'It *really* will not *do*!'
'It *really* will not *do*!'

As the rain on the window-panes turned to sleet Martha often found herself wondering about Mr Jamboree and Madame Wu. Had they turned back again, like Mrs McConkey and the Great Aunts, or were they still birds? And if so, had Mr Jamboree ever reached the warm and balmy shores for which he had set out? And Madame Wu ... What had happened to her? Bantams didn't migrate – Martha was sure of that.

'I do wish I just knew if they were all right,' she said to Mr Teago; but he could give her no assurance. Indeed, he sometimes doubted whether their enchanted summer had ever taken place at all: it all seemed so very far away.

chapter 21

How Martha Made a Happy Discovery

Martha was supposed to come straight home from school the same way every day, and not Dawdle or Gaze in Shop Windows, and never, never Speak to any Strange Man. But one Thursday afternoon, it being Market Day, and also, by a happy coincidence, the Great Aunts' Bridge Afternoon, she decided to come home by way of the market. On bridge afternoons, the Great Aunts never got back till half past six, and when they did they were always so busy arguing about Trumps and Tricks and Aces and things that they had very little time to spare for Martha, so she knew it would be quite safe.

Head down against the wind she hurried along towards the great square. It was a cold and blustery evening, and by the time she got there most of the stall-holders were thankfully packing up their wares and stowing them into their vans, ready for another day in another market place. Martha thought it must be a hard life for them, in spite of their fur boots and woolly mittens and all their overcoats. The fish stall lady seemed to have about six on underneath her apron, and a tartan scarf under her fur hat, but she still had to stamp her feet and fling her arms about her to keep from freezing.

She was too late to do any Christmas shopping: the gift stall had already been taken down and most of the remaining ones were on the point of collapse, but on the far side of the market there was still one standing. She hurried towards it, drawn by the bright light of the hissing lantern and the glow of gay colours from the merchandise within. Above the stall was a painted sign with strange foreign-looking letters; as she drew nearer they revealed it to be, in fact,

THE TAJ MAHAL BAZAAR

She gave a little gasp of surprise: surely Mr Jamboree had talked about the Taj Mahal Bazaar? Wasn't that the name of the stall belonging to his friend – the friend who had lent him the suitcase and the hatstand and all the other things? Perhaps the friend might have some news of him ...

But what if Mr Jamboree *hadn't* changed back? What if he were still a mynah-bird? It would be very difficult to explain. Unless, of course, she just asked if he had any mynah-birds, but then she might end up having to buy one that wasn't Mr Jamboree at all. It was very hard to know what to do.

By this time she was standing right under the canopy, but so lost in thought was she that she scarcely saw the marvellous array of skirts and scarves and saris, of beads and bangles, toys and trays and lamps and ornaments that filled the little stall. And then suddenly the canvas flap at the back moved and there before her very eyes stood – not Mr Jamboree's friend, but Mr Jamboree himself, looking just the same as the first time Martha had seen him, except perhaps a little smarter and perhaps a little fatter.

'Good evening, miss,' he said, smiling charmingly. 'May I perhaps interest you in my very wide range of oriental curiosities? Carved ivory of finest workmanship? Boxes of jade, ebony or sandalwood? Silks and gauzes, delicate as a butterfly's wing? Betel-nuts? Joss-sticks? Brass from Benares? Rich embroideries ...'

'Mr Jamboree!' cried Martha, interrupting him in full flow. 'Oh, Mr Jamboree! I was so worried about you, so was Mr Teago. Have you been all right?'

'Thank you, yes, I have been quite all right. Indeed, quite absolutely. It is not necessary to be worrying on my behalf, although most kind. I trust that you also are keeping quite well?'

'Oh, yes thank you, I'm fine!' said Martha happily. It was really so wonderful to have found him again after such a long time. What adventures he must have had! She longed to hear about them.

'When did you get back?' she asked at last, unable to restrain her curiosity. 'Did you have many adventures?'

Mr Jamboree looked more puzzled than ever.

'On your journey,' Martha explained, '*you* know – to the balmy islands and the palm-grove shores ...'

'Barmy islands?' repeated Mr Jamboree, quite at a loss. 'I am afraid –'

'O-oh,' said Martha, feeling deeply disappointed. So he never got there after all ... 'What a shame,' she said, sighing. 'I suppose it was very difficult to find the way; but Mr Teago and I often and often thought of you, flitting among the coconut palms. We thought it must be so lovely among the coconut pa—'

'Ah, *coconuts*!' said Mr Jamboree, thinking that at last he was beginning to get the drift of Martha's conversation. 'Ah, I regret that we do not stock them at all. You can obtain them at the fruit stall, however. All sizes,' he added helpfully, 'large, medium and small. Very cheap.'

'Oh, no, no, it's quite all right, thank you,' said Martha hastily. 'I don't actually want to *buy* any, not today, anyway.' Even small coconuts were quite heavy, and Mr Teago already had a very adequate supply for the birds, and the conversation seemed somehow to be going in quite the wrong direction. Mr Jamboree didn't appear to understand what she was talking about. But, come to think of it, Mrs McConkey hadn't remembered anything at all about being a hen, nor the Great Aunts, pigeons, so perhaps he, too, had forgotten all about his days as a mynah-bird.

Thinking it best to change the subject she inquired after Madame Wu. 'What became of her after – well, afterwards? Did she just go back to the Magic Shop again?'

At the mention of the Chinawoman's name Mr Jamboree at once became agitated. He glanced nervously to right and left, then he leaned across the counter towards Martha and shook his head in silence.

Martha looked to right and left also, in case perhaps Madame Wu should be shopping in the market, but seeing no sign of her, pursued her inquiries.

'Well, did she?'

'Then you have not heard?' asked Mr Jamboree, in hushed tones.

Martha shook her head. 'Heard what?'

'The Magic Shop ... It has gone.'

'Gone?' said Martha. 'Gone where?'

'Who can say?' said Mr Jamboree, enigmatically. 'You would never know that it had ever existed. It went, as it were, in a puff of smoke, last summer.'

'You mean it caught fire?'

Mr Jamboree did not answer; he was busy taking things down off the rails at the back of the stall and packing them into boxes.

'But what a terrible thing!' went on Martha. 'How did it happen?'

Mr Jamboree shrugged. 'I was not there myself at the time,' he said, 'having been sent on an errand. Possibly it was the firecrackers, they are most dangerous. Also there was much paper lying about at the time, also wood shavings...'

'Wood shavings!' cried Martha, aghast, remembering vividly her last visit to the Magic Shop. 'How *awful*!

And what about the doves and all the rabbits? Were they all burnt too?' It was too dreadful to think of.

'Burnt?' said Mr Jamboree. 'Oh, good gracious goodness, no. They simply disappeared. They were in any case all of the vanishing variety.' And he continued his task of packing up the stall.

'Then what happened to Madame Wu, with no shop to go back to?' Martha asked again. 'You still haven't told me.' She supposed that as everybody else had returned to normal, so had the Chinawoman; but Mr Jamboree seemed disinclined to talk about her, and became busier than ever with his packing. It was getting quite dark and the wind whistled round Martha's legs. She wanted to get home, but was determined to find out about Madame Wu before she went.

'Did she go back to China?'

Mr Jamboree crammed a whole armful of garments into a tea-chest and turned towards Martha, resignedly.

'No,' he said, rather crossly. 'Unfortunately she is not going back to China at all. She is staying here.'

'Here?'

Mr Jamboree nodded briefly. 'She also has a stall in the market.'

'A magic stall?' asked Martha, hopefully.

'Oh, no,' said Mr Jamboree. 'She is quite finished with all that.'

'Then what *does* she sell?' persisted Martha. She was really getting quite impatient with Mr Jamboree.

'Oh,' he said cramming armfuls of garments into a packing case, 'this and that. She is not in a steady line of business at all. One week it is Chop-Suey Take-Away, the next Pekinese dogs; then Chinese Marriage Counsellor. This week it is Pick-your-own-Goldfish. It makes me very nervous, not knowing what to expect. I wish that she would indeed go back to China.'

And with that Mr Jamboree bade Martha good-night and struck camp, so to speak. Disappearing beneath a heap of canvas he ceased business for the day.

chapter 22

How Martha and Mr Teago Went to Market

Mr Teago was overjoyed to hear the good news about Mr Jamboree, though disappointed to learn that he had never reached the coconut isles. The poor fellow had had such a wretched life working for Madame Wu: it had been nice to think that he was having a really good holiday. But at any rate Martha seemed to think that he was quite happy working in the market; apparently he looked both well and prosperous, with a beautiful new turban of peacock hues. Martha had not seen the friend; Mr Jamboree seemed to be in sole charge of the Taj Mahal Bazaar – a position of some importance. Clearly he was doing very well.

But what a terrible thing about the Magic Shop! Poor Martha had been dreadfully upset imagining that it was somehow her fault, though of course the silly child had had nothing to do with the fire, and in any case none of the birds or animals had come to any harm.

And Madame Wu had a stall in the market too! Of course, he had really only known her as a bantam, so it was funny to think of her standing behind a counter. It would be rather amusing to go and see her, and Mr Jamboree as well. He said as much to Martha.

And so it came about that on the following Thursday Mr Teago left his office in the town hall a little early so as to meet Martha as she came out of school.

Together they walked through the darkening, Christ-massy streets, past the bright shop windows filled with tinsel and reindeer and cotton-wool snow, until at last they came to the Market Square. Martha walked ahead, threading her way among the jostling shoppers while Mr Teago followed, pushing his bicycle.

'Jamboree! My dear fellow!' cried Mr Teago warmly when they reached the Taj Mahal Bazaar; but Mr Jamboree was serving a customer and only responded with a rather curt nod and a muttered 'Good evening, sir.'

'Let's go and look for Madame Wu,' said Martha. 'Perhaps he won't be so busy if we come back later.'

They found Madame Wu at last. Not knowing what she might be selling made the search rather difficult, but they discovered her in the end sitting under a large black umbrella doing a brisk trade in roasted chestnuts. Martha and Mr Teago joined the queue of customers and waited patiently while the Chinawoman raked the hot nuts out of the brazier and scooped them into paper bags. Martha was afraid of being recognized, but Madame Wu did not appear to pay the slightest atten-tion to any of her customers, gazing over their heads in a very superior way as she held out her hand for their money.

The chestnuts were extremely hot and painful to peel, but so delicious that it was worth the agony; when they had finished them they went back to Mr Jamboree, but by this time he was busy with more customers so they decided to leave him for another week.

'At least we know he's all right,' said Martha.

'And doing very well, too, by all appearances,' agreed Mr Teago as they turned their steps homeward.

But they had not gone very far when Martha stopped.
'I tell you what,' she said. 'Shall we just go and look at
the Magic Shop? I don't think it's very far.'

'But it was burnt down,' said Mr Teago, who rather
wanted to get home to his tea. 'There won't be anything
to see.'

'There might be,' said Martha.

So he allowed himself to be persuaded and they set
off, Martha leading the way, until they came to the part
of the town where the streets were narrow and cobbled
and the old houses leaned towards each other as if they
were having a good gossip.

'It's down here, I *think*,' said Martha uncertainly.
And on they trudged; but it was difficult to remember
exactly where the Magic Shop had been, especially as it
was no longer there, and of course Mr Teago had never
seen it so he was no help. They walked up one lane and
down another, and Martha kept thinking that she
recognized the street and then kept finding that after all
she didn't, and Mr Teago began to feel very weary. It
was getting awfully dark and rather cold, and the cobbles hurt the soles of his feet and jiggled the things on his
bicycle, causing them to come adrift. He had to keep
stopping to secure them.

'Perhaps we could leave it for now and come back
another day,' he suggested hopefully; but at that
moment Martha gave a cry of recognition and started to
run.

'It's down here!' she cried. 'I know it is. I remember
it now!'

Mr Teago, pushing his bicycle harder than ever,
caught her up.

'Where?' he asked.

'There,' said Martha.

Mr Teago could see nothing: that is, no blackened ruin, no charred timbers open to the sky, no gaunt chimney-pots ...

'I'm sure it was here,' said Martha. 'I *know* it was. I remember *exactly*.'

But there was no sign of it. It was just as Mr Jamboree had said: you would never know that it had existed.

'But it *did* exist!' said Martha vehemently. 'I absolutely remember it all, even the houses on each side of it. Look, that one! And that one! And it was *there* in the middle. It *was*!' she added, seeing the look of disbelief on Mr Teago's face.

But the two houses looked as if they had been propping each other up for several hundred years and there certainly wasn't any room between them for another one, however small and dark and narrow it might have been. But Martha seemed so certain, and so upset about not being able to show it to him, that he did not quite know what to say.

'Come, my dear,' he said at last, 'let's go home now. Perhaps there'll be crumpets for tea.'

He turned his bicycle round and started to push it back the way he had come, but suddenly it stopped and, with a buck and twist, jerked itself out of Mr Teago's hands and fell to the ground with a crash.

'Oh!' cried Martha, running to help. 'Is anything broken? Is your bike all right?' And kneeling down on the cobbles she started to pick up all Mr Teago's bee-bits-and-pieces. It was extraordinary how many there seemed to be, and in the dusk it was quite difficult to find them; however, at last everything was properly stowed aboard the bicycle to Mr Teago's satisfaction and they were able to set off once more.

So at length they reached Number Eleven. Martha opened the back door and went into the kitchen where Mrs McConkey was waiting for them with the kettle singing on the hob and the butter melting into the crumpets. Outside, Mr Teago leaned his bicycle against the back wall and began the business of unloading it. Suddenly they heard him utter a cry of surprise.

'Hullo! What in the world . . . ?'

A moment later he appeared in the doorway holding a large rectangular board, somewhat blackened at the edges as if it had been burnt. There were screw-holes in the corners.

'That must have been what you bumped into,' said Martha. 'I suppose we picked it up in the dark by mistake.' There had been so many oddments scattered about that it was really hardly surprising.

'It's got some writing on it,' said Mr Teago, peering

closely at it and giving it a rub. 'Why, bless my soul! Look what it says.' And he read aloud:

'Madame Wu
Purveyor of Magic
(Wholesale & Retail)
Hats
Rabbits
Wands, etc.
always in stock
Specialist in Oriental Magic
Early Closing Wednesdays.'

'You see!' cried Martha triumphantly, 'I *was* right! I *knew* it was there.' And Mr Teago had to admit that she was indeed absolutely right. There could be no doubt about it.

When tea was over they all sat round the kitchen table and discussed at length what they would do with

the notice: should it go in Martha's bedroom or Mr Teago's carriage? Mrs McConkey would have absolutely nothing to do with it.

While they talked Mr Teago toasted his feet, in their comfortable slippers, in front of the stove; and by and by they recovered from their long tiring afternoon's walk, and slowly, almost imperceptibly began to rise above the hearth...

There are more than 1,000 other titles published in Puffins. Some of them are described on the following pages.

THE MAGIC GRANDFATHER

Jay Williams

Sam was thrilled to discover that his grandfather used magic. Not magic with tricks and sleight of hand, but *real* magic! Then Grandpa disappeared in the middle of a complicated spell and Sam had to work out some way of getting him back. With the help of his cousin Sarah, Sam is suddenly aware that the family talent for magic isn't as dead as Grandpa had thought . . .

THE MIDDLE OF THE SANDWICH

Tim Kennemore

It's too bad that Helen's mother has to go into hospital just now. It means that Helen has to stay with her aunt and attend the village school for a term instead of going straight from her private London school to the local comprehensive. At first it's all pretty difficult, but then Helen starts to find her feet, and does some much-needed growing up.

NOTHING TO BE AFRAID OF

Jan Mark

A hint of a ghost, a cruelly misunderstood message, a secret shed – just three of the elements in this brilliant collection of stories. The characters in Jan Mark's stories are the sort of people who create their own imaginary world of horrors – and then get trapped in it because these are the sorts of horrors that won't go away. They follow you upstairs in the dark and slide under the bed, and there they stay . . .

THE WORLD AROUND THE CORNER

Maurice Gee

When Caroline discovers an old pair of spectacles in her father's junk shop she has no idea how important they are. Even when she puts them on and sees things very differently, she doesn't guess that the safety of another world depends on them. In a race against time, Caroline has to tackle the ghastly Grimbles and keep her promise to return the spectacles to their rightful owners.

SUPER GRAN IS MAGIC

Forrest Wilson

Super Gran wasn't all that bothered about Mr Black's new invention: a small black box that could hypnotize people and animals. But then a rotten stage magician called Mystico thought of the perfect way to make his act more exciting: he'd set a hypnotized Super Gran to work for him. So suddenly Super Gran had to call on all her Super-powers! The fourth book about everyone's favourite senior citizen.

THE SEARCH FOR TREASURE ISLAND

Emma Tennant

How does a modern boy like Sam get drawn into the cunning scheme hatched by Squire Trelawney and his friends to return to Treasure Island in search of more booty? Taking R. L. Stevenson's classic story as its starting point, *The Search for Treasure Island* develops into a marvellous adventure-fantasy with submarines and pirates, cannons and computer banks.

Heard about the Puffin Club?

... it's a way of finding out more about Puffin books and authors, of winning prizes (in competitions), sharing jokes, a secret code, and perhaps seeing your name in print! When you join you get a copy of our magazine, *Puffin Post*, sent to you four times a year, a badge and a membership book.
For details of subscription and an application form, send a stamped addressed envelope to:

The Puffin Club Dept A
Penguin Books Limited
Bath Road
Harmondsworth
Middlesex UB7 ODA

and if you live in Australia, please write to:

The Australian Puffin Club
Penguin Books Australia Limited
P.O. Box 257
Ringwood
Victoria 3134